W9-ALV-556

WAITING
FOR ORDERS

WAITING FOR ORDERS

THE COMPLETE SHORT STORIES OF ERIC AMBLER

ERIC AMBLER

THE MYSTERIOUS PRESS
New York • Tokyo • Sweden • Milan
Published by Warner Books
A Time Warner Company

The stories in this collection are previously published as follows:

"The Army of the Shadows" appeared in *The Queen's Book of the Red Cross*. London: Hodder & Stoughton, Ltd., 1939.

The stories in "The Intrusions of Dr. Czissar" appeared in various issues of *The Sketch* (London), 1940.

"The Blood Bargain" appeared in *Winter's Crime 2*. London: Macmillan, Ltd., 1972.

Mysterious Press books are published by
Warner Books, Inc., 666 Fifth Avenue, New York, NY 10103.

A Time Warner Company

Printed in the United States of America
First printing: February 1991
10 9 8 7 6 5 4 3 2 1

Library of Congress Cataloging-in-Publication Data

Ambler, Eric, 1909–
[Short stories]
Waiting for orders / Eric Ambler.
p. cm.
ISBN 0-89296-241-0
1. Detective and mystery stories, English. I. Title.
PR6001.M48W3 1991
823'.912—dc20 90-50544
CIP

Contents

WAITING
FOR ORDERS

Introduction

Most of these stories were written in haste, one after the other, in the space of a few weeks. I was not a practiced writer of short stories and the reasons for that odd flurry of activity are clearer now than they seemed then. Then I had too many other things on my mind to think clearly about what I wrote—things like love and war and marriage and the fortunes of a new book, *The Mask of Dimitrios*, just out in London as a Book-of-the-Month. The month in question, however, was August 1939; not a good month for books, nor indeed for much else in Europe.

In those days the only Harry's Bar of any note outside Italy was the one in Paris. It was on the rue Blanche just down the hill from Bricktop's, the other friendly night spot within easy walking distance of the Pigalle Métro. My companion in both places was Louise Crombie, fashion artist, born in Portland, Oregon, divorced and working in Paris to support a young family back in New Jersey. On the night of the twenty-second of that month we were drinking brandy *à l'eau* and trying to decide whether to face the complications of an Anglo-American marriage under French law or to go on living together without legal or clerical blessings. There was going to be a war, but what sort of war? Who were going to be the allies against Hitler?

It was to Harry's Bar that night that we went in search of news. There, just after midnight, a man used to come by selling early editions of the morning papers. So, that night, that was how we heard the awful news of the signing of the Molotov-von Ribbentrop non-aggression pact between the Soviet Union and Nazi Germany.

I can still recall the shock of that moment, and the pang of fear that came with it. I was a man of the Popular Front, that short-lived coalition of the European Left against the spread of Axis Fascism that was jumping the frontiers of Versailles Treaty Europe with the remorseless ease of a medieval plague. I believed, with many others, that the Munich Agreement of the year before had been a humiliating disaster, but I had also believed, and also with others, that the Soviet Union would in the end join with the French and British democracies to confront and contain the common enemy. Now, suddenly, there was light on the stage and the hero could be seen climbing into bed with the villain. We did not know then, of course, that the pact signed by Molotov and Ribbentrop had, as well as giving the Nazis a free hand to take anything they wanted of the pre-1914 German territories, secretly partitioned Poland and ceded the Baltic states of Lithuania, Latvia, and Estonia to the Soviet Union; but the fact that Stalin and Hitler had done a deal of any sort was enough. The war, for long inevitable, would now certainly be total.

A few days later we went to London. Our plan was to get married as soon as British law allowed. Louise would then have dual nationality and, if she wanted them, two passports. But several weeks would elapse before the marriage could take place. It was time to think about fighting the war. I was thirty then and if I waited to be called up with my age group I would end up in the army somewhere near the blunt end. Best to volunteer, I thought, and decided to consult my agent. He, I was sure, would have contacts in high places. He had indeed, and soon got my name onto priority lists of volunteers for both the Navy and the RAF. All I had to do then was what everyone else on those lists was doing—wait for orders to report for an interview. Everyone, it seemed, was waiting for orders.

Everyone except my publishers, that is. They had orders from the City of London to compile and produce with all speed a celebratory book. It would be for sale throughout the British Empire and its purpose would be to raise money quickly for the Red Cross. The result was *The Queen's Book of the Red Cross*, a small-quarto volume of three hundred or so pages with a facsimile message from Her Majesty on Buckingham Palace paper and contributions from fifty British authors and artists. It was an expensive book, with color litho and photogravure illustrations to supplement the letterpress text, and a fine cloth board binding. Among the authors who contributed stories were Hugh Walpole, Daphne du Maurier, and A.A. Milne; among the poets were T.S. Eliot and John Masefield; the artists included Laura Knight, Rex

Whistler, and Mabel Lucie Atwell. The most remarkable thing about it, however, was the speed with which the work was done. The whole process from editorial start to finished copies from the binders was accomplished in two months. The dogs of war can start some unusual runners.

The story I contributed was "The Army of the Shadows." I wrote it steadily, cutting and revising as I went as usual, but I wrote with few of the usual hesitations. I had something to say that would soon, I knew, become more difficult to say aloud or plainly: that our enemy was not the German people but the Nazi tyranny to which some of them had submitted. Where better to say it than in a book that was going forth with a royal blessing?

The writing of that story, and perhaps the deadline that went with it, proved oddly stimulating. For the first time since war had been declared I began to think it possible that my career as a writer might not after all be quite over. True, I was waiting for orders and did not want to start a new novel that I might not have time to finish, but I still had the habit of writing every day, a habit I had cultivated and one with which I was always comfortable. When my agent reported that the magazine *The Sketch* wanted to commission from me a series of six very short detective stories, I accepted immediately.

I had never written a detective story of any length, but that did not seem to matter. I had read the great masters of the genre, admired their fearsome ingenuity and enjoyed the literary parlor game they had made of their creation. The Father Brown short stories of G.K. Chesterton had frequently entertained me, not least because of the author's effrontery in endowing his detective with a private line to God. Any approach of mine to the puzzle problem was bound to be less fanciful, but at least it could be workmanlike. I must not disgrace myself by cheating the reader. My plots must work.

That was the week my first orders came. They were to report to Room So-and-So at The Admiralty for an interview. I did and had a bad time. The list my agent had put me on was one for men capable of skippering minesweeping trawlers in the North Sea. The essential qualifications were deep sea yachting experience, membership of a recognized yacht club, and proven ability to navigate. The interviewing officer was a polite bastard with a humiliating smile. I could have murdered him as well as the agent who thought that all writers of thirty could or should be amateur yachtsmen. Instead, I wandered across Trafalgar Square to the Charing Cross Road. There I bought a secondhand copy of Taylor's *Principles and Practice of Medical Jurisprudence*, then the standard general work on the science of forensic medicine.

Taylor came in two volumes. The first dealt with bodily harm resulting from external violence—blows, falls, stabbings, strangulation, fire, gunshot wounds, and other mayhem. The second volume was all about poisons. A couple of days' browsing gave me the technical material for six cosy little murder mysteries; six little puzzles with six solutions that could be explained briefly and without elaborate dissection of alibis. A suitable master detective was needed. He would have to fit into small narrative spaces. His entrances and exits must have a clear pattern. He must belong noticeably to the times we were living in. He must be a refugee.

Dr. Czissar, my refugee Czech detective, was based on two real refugees from Nazi persecution. I had known them both before the war; one a Prague newspaper editor, the other a German historian deprived of his academic post for being part Jewish. The flapping raincoat and the umbrella carried like a rifle were stage props added when I began to write. The historian was the author of a highly praised history of the German army, so it seemed to me right that Czissar should have a soldierly Prussian manner.

The Intrusions of Dr. Czissar passed the time between the more-or-less polite refusal of my services by the Admiralty and their curt rejection by the RAF—"What the hell do you expect us to have for a thirty-year-old writer? Try the army." Louise Crombie and I were married quietly in the local town hall, a civil ceremony conducted by the Registrar of Births, Marriages and Deaths. A certain piquancy was added to the occasion by our being in the possession of inside information. In that London suburb the deaths expected in the first serious air raid would number around five thousand, and collapsible utility coffins to contain the corpses had been ordered by the man who married us. They were already stored in the town hall cellars below us.

My agent, ever alert, had news for me, however. He had discovered by secret means that it would be at least six months before I could expect orders to join the army. Thus, for me, began the period of the phony war. I stopped waiting for orders and took a course in First Aid for stretcher-bearers. I also began to write *Journey into Fear*.

Eleven years went by before I wrote another novel, and thirty before anyone asked me for another short story. The first hiatus is easily explained—war, movie-making, middle age. The second is more difficult. I think I have enjoyed reading short stories more than I could ever have enjoyed writing them; and in the war years the popular short story achieved a late apotheosis. Hemingway, H.E. Bates, and Dorothy Parker are the names that come first to mind, of course, but Irwin Shaw, John Cheever, and Stanley Ellin are the ones that stay with me. Then came television.

The last story in this book is an episode from a failed novel. It was written before the invention of the home shredder and after California brushfires could safely be relied upon to retrieve such indiscretions.

Eric Ambler
London 1990

The Army of the Shadows

It is three years since Llewellyn removed my appendix; but we still meet occasionally. I am dimly related to his wife: that, at least, is the pretext for the acquaintanceship.

The truth is that, during my convalescence, we happened to discover that we both like the same musicians. Before the war we usually met when there was some Sibelius being played and went to hear it together. I was a little puzzled when, about three weeks ago, he telephoned with the suggestion that I should dine at his house that night. There was not, I knew, a concert of any sort in London. I agreed, however, to grope my way round to Upper Wimpole Street shortly before eight o'clock.

It was not until he had presented me with a brandy that I found out why I had been invited to dinner.

"Do you remember," he said suddenly, "that I spent a week or so in Belgrade last year? I missed Beecham doing the Second through it. There was one of those international medical bun fights being held there, and

I went to represent the Association. My German is fairly good, you know. I motored. Can't stick trains. Anyway, on the way back a very funny thing happened to me. Did I ever tell you about it?"

"I don't think so."

"I thought not. Well"—he laughed self-consciously—"it was so funny now there's a war on that I've been amusing myself by writing the whole thing down. I wondered whether you'd be good enough to cast a professional eye over it for me. I've tried"—he laughed again—"to make a really literary job of it. Like a story, you know."

His hand had been out of sight behind the arm of his chair, but now it emerged from hiding holding a wad of typewritten sheets.

"It's typed," he said, planking it down on my knees. And then, with a theatrical glance at his watch, "Good Lord, it's ten. There's a telephone call I must make. Excuse me for a minute or two, will you?"

He was out of the room before I could open my mouth to reply. I was left alone with the manuscript.

I picked it up. It was entitled A Strange Encounter. *With a sigh, I turned over the title page and began, rather irritably, to read:*

The Stelvio Pass is snowed up in winter, and towards the end of November most sensible men driving to Paris from Belgrade or beyond take the long way round via Milan rather than risk being stopped by an early fall of snow. But I was in a hurry and took a chance. By the time I reached Bolzano I was sorry I had done so. It was bitterly cold, and the sky ahead was leaden. At Merano I seriously considered turning back. Instead, I pushed on as hard as I could go. If I had had any sense I should have stopped for petrol before I started the really serious part of the climb. I had six gallons by the gauge then. I knew that it wasn't accurate, but I had filled up early that morning and calculated that I had enough to get me to Sargans. In my anxiety to beat the snow I overlooked the fact that I had miles of low-gear driving to do. On the Swiss side and on the Sargans road where it runs within a mile or two of the Rhätikon part of the German frontier, the car sputtered to a standstill.

For a minute or two I sat there swearing at and to myself and wondering what on earth I was going to do. I was, I knew, the only thing on the road that night for miles.

It was about eight o'clock, very dark and very cold. Except for the faint creaking of the cooling engine and the rustle of the breeze in some nearby trees, there wasn't a sound to be heard. Ahead, the road in the headlights curved away to the right. I got out the map and tried to find out where I was.

I had passed through one village since I had left Klosters, and I knew that it was about ten kilometers back. I must, therefore, either walk back ten kilometers to that village, or forward to the next village, whichever was the nearer. I looked at the map. It was of that useless kind that they sell to motorists. There was nothing marked between Klosters and Sargans. For all I knew, the next village might be fifteen or twenty kilometers away.

An Alpine road on a late November night is not the place to choose if you want to sleep in your car. I decided to walk back the way I had come.

I had a box of those small Italian waxed matches with me when I started out. There were, I thought, about a hundred in the box, and I calculated that, if I struck one every hundred meters, they would last until I reached the village.

That was when I was near the lights of the car. When I got out of sight of them, things were different. The darkness seemed to press against the backs of my eyes. It was almost painful. I could not even see the shape of the road along which I was walking. It was only by the rustling and the smell of resin that I knew that I was walking between fir trees. By the time I had covered a mile I had six matches left. Then it began to snow.

I say, "snow." It had been snow; but the Sargans road was still below the snow-line, and the stuff came down as a sort of half-frozen mush that slid down my face into the gap between my coat collar and my neck.

I must have done about another mile and a half when the real trouble began. I still had the six matches, but my hands were too numb to get them out of the box without wetting them, and I had been going forward blindly, sometimes on the road and sometimes off it. I was wondering whether I would get along better if I sang, when I walked into a telegraph post.

It was of pre-cast concrete and the edge was as sharp as a razor. My face was as numb as my hands and I didn't feel much except a sickening jar; but I could taste blood trickling between my teeth and found that my nose was bleeding. It was as I held my head back to stop it that I saw the light, looking for all the world as if it were suspended in mid-air above me.

It wasn't suspended in mid-air, and it wasn't above me. Darkness does strange things to perspective.

After a few seconds I saw that it was showing through the trees on the hillside, up off the right of the road.

Anyone who has been in the sort of mess that I was in will know exactly how my mind worked at that moment. I did not speculate as to the origin of that God-forsaken light or as to whether or not the owner of it would be pleased to see me. I was cold and wet, my nose was bleeding, and I would not have cared if someone had told me that behind that light was a maniac with a machine-gun. I knew only that the light meant that there was some sort of human habitation near me and that I was going to spend the night in it.

I moved over to the other side of the road and began to feel my way along the wire fence I found there. Twenty yards or so farther on, my hands touched a wooden gate. The light was no longer visible, but I pushed the gate open and walked on into the blackness.

The ground rose steeply under my feet. It was a path of sorts, and soon I stumbled over the beginnings of a flight of log steps. There must have been well over a hundred of them. Then there was another stretch of path, not quite so steep. When I again saw the light, I was only about twenty yards from it.

It came from an oil reading-lamp standing near a window. From the shape of the window and the reflected light of the lamp, I could see that the place was a small chalet of the kind usually let to families for the summer season or for the winter sports. That it should be occupied at the end of November was curious. But I didn't ponder over the curiosity: I had seen something else through the window besides the lamp. The light from a fire was flickering in the room.

I went forward up the path to the door. There was

no knocker. I hammered on the wet, varnished wood with my fist and waited. There was no sound from inside. After a moment or two I knocked again. Still there was no sign of life within. I knocked and waited for several minutes. Then I began to shiver. In desperation I grabbed the latch of the door and rattled it violently. The next moment I felt it give and the door creaked open a few inches.

I think that I have a normal, healthy respect for the property and privacy of my fellow-creatures; but at that moment I was feeling neither normal nor healthy. Obviously, the owner of the chalet could not be far away. I stood there for a moment or two, hesitating. I could smell the wood smoke from the fire, and mingled with it a bitter, oily smell that seemed faintly familiar. But all I cared about was the fire. I hesitated no longer and walked in.

As soon as I was inside I saw that there was something more than curious about the place, and that I should have waited.

The room itself was ordinary enough. It was rather larger than I had expected, but there were the usual pinewood walls, the usual pinewood floor, the usual pinewood staircase up to the bedrooms, and the usual tiled fireplace. There were the usual tables and chairs, too: turned and painted nonsense of the kind that sometimes finds its way into English tea-shops. There were red gingham curtains over the windows. You felt that the owner probably had lots of other places just like it, and that he made a good thing out of letting them.

No, it was what had been added to the room that was curious. All the furniture had been crowded into one half of the space. In the other half, standing on linoleum and looking as if it were used a good deal, was a printing press.

The machine was a small treadle platten of the kind used by jobbing printers for running off tradesmen's circulars. It looked very old and decrepit. Alongside it on a trestle-table were a case of type and a small proofing press with a locked-up forme in it. On a second table stood a pile of interleaved sheets, beside which was a stack of what appeared to be some of the same sheets folded. The folding was obviously being done by hand. I picked up one of the folded sheets.

It looked like one of those long, narrow, business-promotion folders issued by travel agencies. The front page was devoted to the reproduction, in watery blue ink, of a lino-cut of a clump of pines on the shore of a lake, and the display of the word TITISEE. Page two and the page folded in to face it carried a rhapsodical account in German of the beauties of Baden in general and Lake Titisee in particular.

I put the folder down. An inaccessible Swiss chalet was an odd place to choose for printing German travel advertisements; but I was not disposed to dwell on its oddity. I was cold.

I was moving towards the fire when my eye was caught by five words printed in bold capitals on one of the unfolded sheets on the table: "DEUTSCHE MÄNNER UND FRAUEN, KAMERADEN!"

I stood still. I remember that my heart thudded against my ribs as suddenly and violently as it had earlier that day on the Stelvio when some crazy fool in a Hispano had nearly crowded me off the road.

I leaned forward, picked the folder up again, and opened it right out. The message began on the second of the three inside pages.

"German Men and Women, Comrades! We speak to you with the voice of German Democracy, bringing you news. Neither Nazi propaganda nor the Gestapo can silence us, for we have an ally which is proof against floggings, an ally which no man in the history of the world has been able to defeat. That ally is Truth. Hear then, people of Germany, the Truth which is concealed from you. Hear it, remember it, and repeat it. The sooner the Truth is known, the sooner will Germany again hold up its head among the free nations of the world."

Then followed a sort of news bulletin consisting chiefly of facts and figures (especially figures) about the economic condition of Germany. There was also news of a strike in the Krupp works at Essen and a short description of a riot outside a shipyard in Hamburg.

I put it down again. Now I knew why these "travel advertisements" were being printed in an inaccessible Swiss chalet instead of in Germany itself. No German railway official would distribute these folders. That business would be left to more desperate men. These folders would not collect dust on the counters of travel agencies. They would be found in trains and in trams, in buses and in parked cars, in waiting-rooms and in bars, under restaurant plates and inside table napkins. Some of the men that put them there would be caught and tortured to betray their fellows; but the distribution would go on. The folders would be read, perhaps furtively discussed. A little more truth would seep through Goebbels' dam of lies to rot still further the creaking foundations of Nazidom.

Then, as I stood there with the smell of wood smoke and printing ink in my nostrils, as I stood staring at that decrepit little machine as if it were the very voice of freedom, I heard footsteps outside.

I suppose that I should have stood my ground. I had, after all, a perfectly good explanation of my presence there. My car and the blood from my nose would confirm my story. But I didn't reason that way. I had stumbled on a secret, and my first impulse was to try to hide the fact from the owner of the secret. I obeyed that impulse.

I looked round quickly and saw the stairs. Before I had even begun to wonder if I might not be doing something excessively stupid, I was up the stairs and opening the first door I came to on the landing. In the half-light I caught a glimpse of a bed; then I was inside the room with the door slightly ajar. I could see across the landing and through the wooden palings along it to the top of the window at the far side of the room below.

I knew that someone had come in: I could hear him moving about. He lit another lamp. There was a sound from the door and a second person entered.

A woman's voice said in German, "Thank God, Johann has left a good fire."

There was an answering grunt. It came from the man. I could almost feel them warming their hands.

"Get the coffee, Freda," said the man suddenly. "I must go back soon."

"But Bruno is there. You should take a little rest first."

"Bruno is a Berliner. He is not as used to the cold as I am. If Kurt should come now he would be tired. Bruno could only look after himself."

There was silence for a moment. Then the woman spoke again.

"Do you really think that he will come now, Stephan? It is so late." She paused. Her voice had sounded casual, elaborately casual; but now, as she went on, there was an edge to it that touched the nerves. "I can keep quite calm about it, you see, Stephan. I wish to believe, but it is so late, isn't it? You don't think he will come now, do you? Admit it."

He laughed, but too heartily. "You are too nervous, Freda. Kurt can take care of himself. He knows all the tricks now. He may have been waiting for the first snow. The frontier guards would not be so alert on a night like this."

"He should have been back a week ago. You know that as well as I do, Stephan. He has never been delayed so long before. They have got him. That is all. You see, I can be calm about it even though he is my dear husband." And then her voice broke. "I knew it would happen sooner or later. I knew it. First Hans, then Karl, and now Kurt. Those swine, those—"

She sobbed and broke suddenly into passionate weeping. He tried helplessly to comfort her.

I had heard enough. I was shaking from head to foot; but whether it was the cold or not, I don't know. I stood back from the door. Then, as I did so, I heard a sound from behind me.

I had noticed the bed as I had slipped into the room, but the idea that there might be someone in it had not entered my head. Now, as I whipped round, I saw that I had made a serious mistake.

Sitting on the edge of the bed in which he had been lying was a very thin, middle-aged man in a nightshirt. By the faint light from the landing I could see his eyes, bleary from sleep, and his grizzled hair standing ludicrously on end. But for one thing I should have laughed. That one thing was the large automatic pistol that he held pointed at me. His hand was as steady as a rock.

"Don't move," he said. He raised his voice. "Stephan! Come quickly!"

"I must apologize . . ." I began in German.

"You will be allowed to speak later."

I heard Stephan dash up the stairs.

"What is it, Johann?"

"Come here."

The door was pushed open behind me. I heard him draw in his breath sharply.

"Who is it?"

"I don't know. I was awakened by a noise. I was about to get up when this man came into the room. He did not see me. He has been listening to your conversation. He must have been examining the plant when he heard you returning."

"If you will allow me to explain . . ."

"You may explain downstairs," said the man called Stephan. "Give me the pistol, Johann."

The pistol changed hands and I could see Stephan, a lean, rawboned fellow with broad, sharp shoulders and dangerous eyes. He wore black oilskins and gum-boots. I saw the muscles in his cheeks tighten.

"Raise your hands and walk downstairs. Slowly. If you run, I shall shoot immediately. March."

I went downstairs.

The woman, Freda, was standing by the door, staring blankly up at me as I descended. She must have been about thirty and had that soft rather matronly look about her that is characteristic of so many young German women. She was short and plump, and as if to accentuate the fact, her straw-colored hair was plaited across her head. Wisps of the hair had become detached and clung wetly to the sides of her neck. She too wore a black oilskin coat and gum-boots.

The gray eyes, red and swollen with crying, looked beyond me.

"Who is it, Stephan?"

"He was hiding upstairs."

We had reached the foot of the stairs. He motioned me away from the door and towards the fire. "Now, we will hear your explanation."

I gave it with profuse apologies. I admitted that I had examined the folders and read one. "It seemed to me," I concluded, "that my presence might be embarrassing to you. I was about to leave when you returned. Then, I am afraid, I lost my head and attempted to hide."

Not one of them was believing a word that I was saying: I could see that from their faces. "I assure you," I went on in exasperation, "that what I am telling . . ."

"What nationality are you?"

"British. I . . ."

"Then speak English. What were you doing on this road?"

"I am on my way home from Belgrade. I crossed the Yugoslav frontier yesterday and the Italian frontier at Stelvio this afternoon. My passport was stamped at both places if you wish to . . ."

"Why were you in Belgrade?"

"I am a surgeon. I have been attending an international medical convention there."

"Let me see your passport, please."

"Certainly. I have . . ." And then with my hand in

my inside pocket, I stopped. My heart felt as if it had come right into my throat. In my haste to be away after the Italian Customs had finished with me, I had thrust my passport with the Customs carnet for the car into the pocket beside me on the door of the car.

They were watching me with expressionless faces. Now, as my hand reappeared empty, I saw Stephan raise his pistol.

"Well?"

"I am sorry." Like a fool I had begun to speak in German again. "I find that I have left my passport in my car. It is several kilometers along the road. If . . ."

And then the woman burst out as if she couldn't stand listening to me any longer.

"Don't you see? Don't you see?" she cried. "It is quite clear. They have found out that we are here. Perhaps after all these months Hans or Karl has been tortured by them into speaking. And so they have taken Kurt and sent this man to spy upon us. It is clear. Don't you see?"

She turned suddenly, and I thought she was going to attack me. Then Stephan put his hand on her arm.

"Gently, Freda." He turned to me again, and his expression hardened. "You see, my friend, what is in our minds? We know our danger, you see. The fact that we are in Swiss territory will not protect us if the Gestapo should trace us. The Nazis, we know, have little respect for frontiers. The Gestapo have none. They would murder us here as confidently as they would if we were in the Third Reich. We do not underrate their cunning. The fact that you are not a German is not conclusive. You may be what you say you are; you may not. If you are, so much the better.

If not, then, I give you fair warning, you will be shot. You say that your passport is in your car several kilometers along the road. Unfortunately, it is not possible for us to spare time tonight to see if that is true. Nor is it possible for one of us to stand guard over you all night. You have already disturbed the first sleep Johann has had in twenty-four hours. There is only one thing for it, I'm afraid. It is undignified and barbaric; but I see no other way. We shall be forced to tie you up so that you cannot leave."

"But this is absurd," I cried angrily. "Good heavens, man, I realize that I've only myself to blame for being here; but surely you could have the common decency to . . ."

"The question," he said sternly, "is not of decency, but of necessity. We have no time tonight for six-kilometer walks. One of our comrades has been delivering a consignment of these folders to our friends in Germany. We hope and believe that he will return to us across the frontier tonight. He may need our help. Mountaineering in such weather is exhausting. Freda, get me some of the cord we use for tying the packages."

I wanted to say something, but the words would not come. I was too angry. I don't think that I've ever been so angry in my life before.

She brought the cord. It was thick gray stuff. He took it and gave the pistol to Johann. Then he came towards me.

I don't think they liked the business any more than I did. He had gone a bit white and he wouldn't look me in the eyes. I think that I must have been white myself; but it was anger with me. He put the cord under one of my elbows. I snatched it away.

"You had better submit," he said harshly.

"To spare your feelings? Certainly not. You'll have to use force, my friend. But don't worry. You'll get used to it. You'll be a good Nazi yet. You should knock me down. That'll make it easier."

What color there was left in his face went. A good deal of my anger evaporated at that moment. I felt sorry for the poor devil. I really believe that I should have let him tie me up. But I never knew for certain; for at that moment there was an interruption.

It was the woman who heard it first—the sound of someone running up the path outside. The next moment a man burst wildly into the room.

Stephan had turned. "Bruno! What is it? Why aren't you at the hut?"

The man was striving to get his breath, and for a moment he could hardly speak. His face above the streaming oilskins was blue with cold. Then he gasped out, "Kurt! He is at the hut! He is wounded—badly!"

The woman gave a little whimpering cry and her hands went to her face. Stephan gripped the newcomer's shoulder.

"What has happened? Quickly!"

"It was dark. The Swiss did not see him. It was one of our patrols. They shot him when he was actually on the Swiss side. He was wounded in the thigh. He crawled on to the hut, but he can go no farther. He . . ."

But Stephan had ceased to listen. He turned sharply. "Johann, you must dress yourself at once. Bruno, take the pistol and guard this man. He broke in here. He may be dangerous. Freda, get the cognac and the iodine. We shall need them for Kurt."

He himself went to a cupboard and got out some handkerchiefs, which he began tearing feverishly into strips, which he knotted together. Still gasping for breath, the man Bruno had taken the pistol and was staring at me with a puzzled frown. Then the woman reappeared from the kitchen carrying a bottle of cognac and a small tube of iodine of the sort that is sold for dabbing at cut fingers. Stephan stuffed them in his pockets with the knotted handkerchiefs. Then he called up the stairs, "Hurry, Johann. We are ready to leave."

It was more than I could bear. Professional fussiness, I suppose.

"Has any one of you," I asked loudly, "ever dealt with a bullet wound before?"

They stared at me. Then Stephan glanced at Bruno.

"If he moves," he said, "shoot." He raised his voice again. "Johann!"

There was an answering cry of reassurance.

"Has it occurred to you," I persisted, "that even if you get him here alive, which I doubt, as you obviously don't know what you're doing, he will need immediate medical attention? Don't you think that one of you had better go for a doctor? Ah, but of course; the doctor would ask questions about a bullet wound, wouldn't he? The matter would be reported to the police."

"We can look after him," he grunted. "Johann! Hurry!"

"It seems a pity," I said reflectively, "that one brave man should have to die because of his friends' stupidity." And then my calm deserted me. "You damn fool!" I shouted. "Listen to me. Do you want to kill this man? You're going about it the right way. I'm a surgeon, and this is a surgeon's business. Take that cognac out of your pocket. We shan't need it. The iodine too. And those pieces of rag. Have you got two or three clean towels?"

The woman nodded stupidly.

"Then get them, please, and be quick. And you said something about some coffee. Have you a flask for it? Good. Then we shall take that. Put plenty of sugar in it. I want blankets, too. Three will be enough, but they must be kept dry. We shall need a stretcher. Get two poles or broomsticks and two old coats. We can make a stretcher of sorts by putting the poles through the sleeves of them. Take this cord of yours too. It will be useful to make slings for the stretcher. And hurry! The man may be bleeding to death. Is he far away?"

The man was glowering at me. "Four kilometers. In a climbing hut in the hills this side of the frontier." He stepped forward and gripped my arm. "If you are tricking us . . ." he began.

"I'm not thinking about you," I snapped. "I'm thinking about a man who's been crawling along with a bullet in his thigh and a touching faith in his friends. Now get those poles, and hurry."

They hurried. In three minutes they had the things collected. The exhausted Bruno's oilskins and gum-boots had, at my suggestion, been transferred to me. Then I tied one of the blankets round my waist under my coat, and told Stephan and Johann to do the same.

"I," said the woman, "will take the other things."

"You," I said, "will stay here, please."

She straightened up at that. "No," she said firmly. "I will come with you. I shall be quite calm. You will see."

"Nevertheless," I said rather brutally, "you will be

more useful here. A bed must be ready by the fire here. There must also be hot bricks and plenty of blankets. I shall need, besides, both boiled and boiling water. You have plenty of ordinary salt, I suppose?"

"Yes, *Herr Doktor*. But . . ."

"We are wasting time."

Two minutes later we left.

I shall never forget that climb. It began about half a mile along the road below the chalet. The first part was mostly up narrow paths between trees. They were covered with pine needles and, in the rain, as slippery as the devil. We had been climbing steadily for about half an hour when Stephan, who had been leading the way with a storm lantern, paused.

"I must put out the light here," he said. "The frontier is only three kilometers from here, and the guards patrol to a depth of two kilometers. They must not see us." He blew out the lamp. "Turn round," he said then. "You will see another light."

I saw it, far away below us, a pin-point.

"That's our light. When we are returning from Germany, we can see it from across the frontier and know that we are nearly home and that our friends are waiting. Hold on to my coat now. You need not worry about Johann behind you. He knows the path well. This way, *Herr Doktor*."

It was the only sign he gave that he had decided to accept me for what I said I was.

I cannot conceive of how anyone could know that path well. The surface soon changed from pine needles to a sort of rocky rubble, and it twisted and turned like a wounded snake. The wind had dropped, but it was colder than ever, and I found myself crunching through sugary patches of half-frozen slush. I wondered how on earth we were going to bring down a wounded man on an improvised stretcher.

We had been creeping along without the light for about twenty minutes when Stephan stopped and, shielding the lamp with his coat, relit it. I saw that we had arrived.

The climbing hut was built against the side of an overhanging rock face. It was about six feet square inside, and the man was lying diagonally across it on his face. There was a large bloodstain on the floor beneath him. He was semi-conscious. His eyes were closed, but he mumbled something as I felt for his pulse.

"Will he live?" whispered Stephan.

I didn't know. The pulse was there, but it was feeble and rapid. His breathing was shallow. I looked at the wound. The bullet had entered on the inner side of the left thigh just below the groin. There was a little bleeding, but it obviously hadn't touched the femoral artery and, as far as I could see, the bone was all right. I made a dressing with one of the towels and tied it in place with another. The bullet could wait. The immediate danger was from shock aggravated by exposure. I got to work with the blankets and the flask of coffee. Soon the pulse strengthened a little, and after about half an hour I told them how to prepare the stretcher.

I don't know how they got him down that path in the darkness. It was all I could do to get down by myself. It was snowing hard now in great fleecy chunks that blinded you when you moved forward. I was prepared for them to slip and drop the stretcher; but they didn't. It was slow work, however, and it was a good forty minutes before we got to the point where it was safe to light the lamp.

After that I was able to help with the stretcher. At the foot of the path up to the chalet, I went ahead with the lantern. The woman heard my footsteps and came to the door. I realized that we must have been gone for the best part of three hours.

"They're bringing him up," I said. "He'll be all right. I shall need your help now."

She said, "The bed is ready." And then, "Is it serious, *Herr Doktor*?"

"No." I didn't tell her then that there was a bullet to be taken out.

It was a nasty job. The wound itself wasn't so bad. The bullet must have been pretty well spent, for it had lodged up against the bone without doing any real damage. It was the instruments that made it difficult. They came from the kitchen. He didn't stand up to it very well, and I wasn't surprised. I didn't feel so good myself when I'd finished. The cognac came in useful after all.

We finally got him to sleep about five.

"He'll be all right now," I said.

The woman looked at me and I saw the tears begin to trickle down her cheeks. It was only then that I remembered that she wasn't a nurse, but his wife.

It was Johann who comforted her. Stephan came over to me.

"We owe you a great debt, *Herr Doktor*," he said. "I must apologize for our behavior earlier this evening. We have not always been savages, you know. Kurt was a professor of zoology. Johann was a master printer. I was an architect. Now we are those who crawl across frontiers at night and plot like criminals. We have been treated like savages, and so we live like them. We forget sometimes that we were civilized. We ask your pardon. I do not know how we can repay you for what you have done. We . . ."

But I was too tired for speeches. I smiled quickly at him.

"All that I need by way of a fee is another glass of cognac and a bed to sleep in for a few hours. I suggest, by the way, that you get a doctor in to look at the patient later today. There will be a little fever to treat. Tell the doctor he fell upon his climbing axe. He won't believe you, but there'll be no bullet for him to be inquisitive about. Oh, and if you could find me a little petrol for my car . . ."

It was five in the afternoon and almost dark again when Stephan woke me. The local doctor, he reported, as he set an enormous tray of food down beside the bed, had been, dressed the wound, prescribed, and gone. My car was filled up with petrol and awaited me below if I wished to drive to Zürich that night. Kurt was awake and could not be prevailed upon to sleep until he had thanked me.

They were all there, grouped about the bed, when I went downstairs. Bruno was the only one who looked as if he had had any sleep.

He sprang to his feet. "Here, Kurt," he said facetiously, "is the *Herr Doktor*. He is going to cut your leg off."

Only the woman did not laugh at the jest. Kurt himself was smiling when I bent over to look at him.

He was a youngish-looking man of about forty with intelligent brown eyes and a high, wide forehead. The smile faded from his face as he looked at me.

"You know what I wish to say, *Herr Doktor*?"

I took refuge in professional brusqueness. "The less you say, the better," I said, and felt for his pulse. But as I did so his fingers moved and gripped my hand.

"One day soon," he said, "England and the Third Reich will be at war. But you will not be at war with Germany. Remember that, please, *Herr Doktor*. Not with Germany. It is people like us who are Germany, and in our way we shall fight with England. You will see."

I left soon after.

At nine that night I was in Zürich.

Llewellyn was back in the room. I put the manuscript down. He looked across at me.

"Very interesting," I said.

"I'd considered sending it up to one of these magazines that publish short stories," he said apologetically. "I thought I'd like your opinion first, though. What do you think?"

I cleared my throat. "Well, of course, it's difficult to say. Very interesting, as I said. But there's no real point to it, is there? It needs something to tie it all together."

"Yes, I see what you mean. It sort of leaves off, doesn't it? But that's how it actually happened." He looked disappointed. "I don't think I could invent an ending. It would be rather a pity, wouldn't it? You see, it's all true."

"Yes, it would be a pity."

"Well, anyway, thanks for reading it. Funny thing to happen. I really only put it down on paper for fun. Have another brandy?" He got up. "Oh, by the way. I was forgetting. I heard from those people about a

week after war broke out. A letter. Let's see now, where did I put it? Ah, yes."

He rummaged in a drawer for a bit, and then, tossing a letter over to me, picked up the brandy bottle.

The envelope bore a Swiss stamp and the postmark was Klosters, September 4th, 1939. The contents felt bulky. I drew them out.

The cause of the bulkiness was what looked like a travel agent's folder doubled up to fit the envelope. I straightened it. On the front page was a lino-cut of a clump of pines on the shore of a lake and the word TITISEE. *I opened out the folder.*

"GERMAN MEN AND WOMEN, COMRADES!" *The type was worn and battered.* "Hitler has led you into war. He fed you with lies about the friendly Polish people. In your name he has now committed a wanton act of aggression against them. As a consequence, the free democracies of England and France have declared war against Germany. Comrades, right and justice are on their side. It is Hitler and National Socialism who are the enemies of peace in Europe. Our place as true Germans is at the side of the democracies *against* Hitler, *against* National Socialism. Hitler cannot win this war. But the people of Germany must act. All Germans, Catholics, Protestants, and Jews, must act now. Our Czech and Slovak friends are already refusing to make guns for Hitler. Let us stand by their sides. Remember . . ."

I was about to read on when I saw that the letter that accompanied the folder had fluttered to the carpet. I picked it up. It consisted of a few typewritten lines on an otherwise blank sheet of paper.

"Greetings, *Herr Doktor*. We secured your address from the Customs carnet in your car and write now to wish you good luck. Kurt, Stephan, and Bruno have made many journeys since we saw you and returned safely each time. Today, Kurt leaves again. We pray for him as always. With this letter we send you Johann's newest work so that you shall see that Kurt spoke the truth to you. We are of the army of the shadows. We do not fight for you against our countrymen; but we fight with you against National Socialism, our common enemy.

"*Auf Wiedersehen*.
"FREDA, KURT, STEPHAN, JOHANN, AND BRUNO."

Llewellyn put my glass down on the table beside me. "Help yourself to a cigarette. What do you think of that? Nice of them, wasn't it?" he added. "Sentimental lot, these Germans."

THE INTRUSIONS OF DR. CZISSAR

1 / The Case of the Pinchbeck Locket

The winter afternoon on which Dr. Jan Czissar chose to introduce his peculiar personality into the life of Assistant-Commissioner Mercer of Scotland Yard was cold and depressing. And Mercer, besides having a cold and being depressed, was also busy. Had Dr. Czissar not been in the possession of a letter of introduction from, as Sergeant Flecker put it, "one of the 'Ome Office brass 'ats," he would not have seen the Assistant-Commissioner at all.

The letter was brief. Having presented his compliments, the writer said that Dr. Jan Czissar had been, until the September of 1938, a distinguished member of the Czech police organization; that he was a welcome guest in this country, and that any courtesy which could be extended to him by the Assistant-Commissioner would be very much appreciated. It was not until it was too late to save himself that Mercer found that the letter, though brief, was by no means to the point.

Mercer had dealt with distinguished visitors to

Scotland Yard before. There would be the preliminary exchange of courtesies, then a tour of the buildings, conducted by Inspector Denton, who would appear, as if by accident, a few moments after the visitor had entered Mercer's room, and, finally, the farewell handshake and a safe conduct to the Embankment entrance and a taxi.

In spite, therefore, of his cold and his depression and his interrupted work, it was with a smile that Mercer greeted Dr. Czissar's entry into his room.

Dr. Czissar was a plump, middle-aged man of rather more than medium height, with a round, pale face and a pair of sad, brown eyes, magnified to cow-like proportions by a pair of thick pebble glasses. He wore a long gray raincoat, which reached nearly to his ankles, and carried an unfurled umbrella. As he came into the room he stopped, clicked his heels, clapped the umbrella to his side as if it were a rifle, bowed, and said loudly and distinctly: "Doctor Jan Czissar. Late Prague police. At your service."

"Delighted, Doctor. Won't you take a seat?"

Dr. Czissar took a seat. His cow-like eyes blinked round the room and came to rest once more on Mercer.

"It is good of you," said the Doctor suddenly, "to see me so promptly. It is an honor to be received at Scotland Yard. In common with my colleagues"—the cow-like eyes narrowed slightly—"my *late* colleagues of the Czech police, I have always admired your institution."

Mercer was used to dealing with this sort of thing. He smiled deprecatingly. "We do our best. Ours is a law-abiding country." And then his ears caught the sound they had been waiting for—the sound of Inspector Denton's footsteps approaching along the corridor. He rose to his feet. "Well, Doctor, now that you're here, I expect you'd like to see something of our organization, eh?"

Time had given the question a purely rhetorical significance for Mercer. For him, Dr. Czissar was already safely under the wing of the approaching Inspector Denton. The words of introduction were already rising to his lips, the Inspector was already rapping dutifully at the door, the machinery for the speedy disposal of distinguished visitors was getting smoothly under way: and then, the unbelievable happened.

Dr. Czissar said: "Oh no, thank you. I will not trouble."

For a moment Mercer thought that he had misunderstood.

"It's no trouble at all, Doctor."

"Some other day, perhaps." The cow-like eyes regarded him kindly. "I am rather busy, you know. A text-book of medical jurisprudence. Perhaps if we could have a little talk about an important matter in which I am interested it would be better."

Mercer subsided slowly into his chair. He saw Denton was standing helplessly inside the door. He heard Sergeant Flecker, at his desk in the corner, say "Crikey!" a little too loudly. Dr. Czissar's large, sad eyes regarded him compassionately. He strove to render his face and voice expressionless.

"Well, Doctor. What can we do for you?"

"Pardon, Assistant-Commissioner Mercer. It is I who can do something for you."

"Ah, yes?"

And then Mercer witnessed, for the first of many

times, the spectacle of Dr. Czissar going into action. A faint, thin smile stretched the Doctor's full lips. He settled his glasses on his nose. Then he produced an enormous alligator-skin wallet and took from it a newspaper cutting. Finally, he performed a series of three actions which Mercer was going in time to recognize and to detest. He cleared his throat, swallowed hard, and then said sharply: "Attention, please!"

"I think," he added slowly, "that I can help you to discover a crime. Clever criminals are so stupid, are they not?"

Mercer stroked his chin. A warm, comfortable feeling suffused his breast. This Czech was just another lunatic, after all. Unhinged, no doubt, by his experiences as a refugee. He thought of the memorandum he would send the "brass hat" in the Home Office and smiled benignly on Dr. Czissar. Once more he got to his feet.

"Very good of you. Now, if you'll just put the whole thing in writing and post it to me, we'll look into it."

Dr. Czissar's thin smile vanished. The cow-like eyes flashed. "It is unnecessary. The matter is in writing and here." He put the newspaper cutting under Mercer's nose. "Please," he said firmly, "to read."

Again Mercer sat down. His eyes met those of Dr. Czissar. He read.

The cutting was from a Wessex weekly newspaper dated a fortnight previously, and was the report of an inquest. The body of a woman of sixty had been washed up in Shingles Bay and had been identified as that of Mrs. Sarah Fallon, of Seahurst, a village five miles from the seaside resort of Seabourne. Her husband had died fifteen years earlier, leaving her a large fortune and Seahurst Grange, with its twenty-acre park. Soon after his death she had assumed the guardianship of his niece, Helen Fallon, who had married, eleven years later, Arthur Barrington, a Seabourne coal and builders' merchant, and President of the Seabourne Angling Society. The Barringtons had lived since their marriage with Mrs. Fallon at the Grange.

On the evening of November 4 Barrington had reported to the police that Mrs. Fallon had disappeared. That afternoon Mrs. Barrington had, at her aunt's request, driven her into Seabourne to do some shopping. As Mrs. Fallon had said that she might call on a friend for tea, her niece had left her at South Square at a quarter to three, put the car in the municipal car park, and spent the afternoon in a cinema. They had arranged to meet at South Square at six o'clock. Mrs. Fallon had not kept the appointment, and later, when attempts to trace her movements through her friends had failed, the police had been informed.

She had not been seen again until eight days later, when her body was found by a coastguard.

Evidence of identification was given by her doctor and her dentist. The post-mortem had revealed the cause of death as being shock following a fracture of the skull. The fracture could have been caused by violent contact with any blunt, hard surface. It would have been consistent with a fall from a high cliff. She had not entered the water until several hours after death. The state of decomposition suggested that she had probably died on the date of her disappearance. Her doctor added that she had suffered from a cardiac disturbance and was liable to spells of dizziness.

A child, Annie Smith, had given evidence of the

finding, on the seventh of the month, of a heart-shaped pinchbeck locket at the foot of Sea Head Cliff, a local beauty spot within a few minutes' walk of South Square.

Mrs. Barrington had identified the locket as having belonged to her aunt. Her aunt, who had attached great sentimental value to the locket, had always worn it. Her aunt had been in the habit of sitting on the seat on the cliff during the afternoon. She had not, however, done so for several days prior to her disappearance as she had had a cold.

The coroner, summing up, had said that there seemed very little doubt that the deceased had, after she had left her niece on the afternoon of the fourth, changed her mind about visiting her friends and walked up the hill to the cliff. Then, fatigued by the walk after her recent illness, she had had an attack of giddiness and fallen to her death on the beach below. High tide had been at six o'clock. Her body must have lain on the beach until ultimately it had been carried out to sea.

A verdict of "Accidental Death" had been returned, the jury adding a rider to the effect that the cliff should be fenced.

Mercer looked up. "Well, Doctor?"

"Mrs. Fallon," said Dr. Czissar decisively, "was, I think, murdered."

Mercer sighed and leaned back in his chair.

"Sergeant," he said, "get me the file on the Fallon case, will you?" He smiled wearily at the Doctor. "You see, Doctor we are not so stupid. A rich woman meets with an accident. Her niece, who lives in her house, inherits. The niece's husband, who also lives in the house, happens to be in financial difficulties in his business. The Chief Constable of Wessex thought it advisable to ask us to look into the matter. Ah, thank you, Sergeant. Here we are, Doctor. All open and above-board. The niece first.

"She spent the afternoon as she says she did. Car-park and cinema attendants both confirm that she spent the afternoon at Seabourne. She arrived home at seven, having waited for half an hour in South Square and spent ten minutes or so telephoning her aunt's friends. Barrington returned home soon afterwards. He had left at two-thirty to keep a business appointment in Haywick—that's fourteen miles farther west along the coast—at three. He kept the appointment, and several others that he had made in the Haywick district for that afternoon. Anyway, no murderer in his senses would try to push anybody off the cliff. There's a coastguard station a quarter of a mile away. He would be too scared of being seen. Satisfied, Doctor?"

Dr. Czissar's thin smile had reappeared. He nodded. "Oh, yes. Quite satisfied. She was undoubtedly murdered. Were the servants at the Grange questioned?"

Mercer swallowed hard. "Naturally."

"And did any of them report any trouble with the heating arrangements on the night of Mrs. Fallon's disappearance?"

Mercer restrained himself with an effort. He turned slowly to Inspector Denton. "Well, Inspector? You went down to Seahurst, didn't you? Can you answer the Doctor's question? By the way," he added perfunctorily, "this is Inspector Denton, Doctor."

Dr. Czissar sprang up like a Jack-in-the-box, clicked his heels, and sat down again.

The Inspector shifted uneasily. "As a matter of fact," he said, averting his eyes from his superior, "there was some trouble with the heating, Sir. The housekeeper's a spiritualist, Sir, like myself, and she said they had trouble with the furnace that night. It went out. She reckoned that it was a sort of sign that the old lady had pegged out. Died," he added by way of explanation, and relapsed into uncomfortable silence.

"Ah, so!" said Dr. Czissar. His sad, brown eyes fastened again on Mercer's. "Do you begin to see my argument, Assistant-Commissioner?"

Mercer stirred. "To be frank with you, Doctor," he said, "I think that we are both wasting time."

Dr. Czissar smiled serenely. "Attention, please," he said. "I will present the case to you."

He raised one finger. "First," he said, "the thing that attracts my attention is this matter of the locket. So curious, I think. It is found at the bottom of the cliff. Therefore, Mrs. Fallon was killed by falling from the cliff. So simple. Perhaps a little *too* simple, do you think? It is found three days after the accident. Therefore it must have fallen on a place not covered by the tide. Six tides would certainly have buried it or swept it away, don't you think? Yesterday I went to Seabourne. I looked at the cliff. So interesting. It is quite impossible to drop an object from the top of the cliff so that it lands on the beach above the high-tide mark."

Mercer shrugged. "The clasp was broken. She probably clutched at it as she fell. She had heart trouble. It would be a natural gesture. It might fall anywhere under the circumstances."

The brown eyes remained cow-like, but the full lips curled a little. "Ah, so! It might. A woman of sixty in a poor state of health might also climb to the top of the cliff on a cold November day and stand near enough to the edge to fall over. But it is unlikely. And was she seen by the coastguards?"

"No. But that proves nothing. I think I should tell you, too, that the fact that she was washed up in Shingles Bay confirms the theory that she entered the water by the cliff. The currents are very strong there. From the cliff she would be certain to find her way to the bay."

"Ah! She arrives in the Shingles Bay. Therefore she must have come from the cliff. Is that right?"

"There is the evidence of the locket."

"Attention, please." The thin smile had returned once more. "I have made certain inquiries in Seabourne."

"Indeed?"

"About the currents. You are, within limits, correct. There is a very strong current running past the cliff and across Firth Bay to the Shingles. But"—the eyes approached Mercer's quickly—"this current sweeps along near the coast for some distance. It goes in very near to the coast at Haywick Dunes. And does it not occur to you, too, that eight days is a long time for a body to take to get from the cliff to Shingles Bay? The current is, as you said, a strong one."

Mercer looked at Denton. "Were we aware of these facts, Inspector?"

"No, Sir. The local men were quite sure about the cliff. They said they'd had one or two suicides from there and that the bodies all ended up in Shingles Bay."

"I see. May I ask where you obtained this information, Doctor?"

"From the Secretary of the Seabourne Angling Society." Dr. Czissar coughed gently. "Mr. Barrington is the President of the Society this year, according to the newspaper. He, too, would know these things."

"I see. Well, Doctor, this is very interesting, but I am afraid—"

"Mrs. Fallon," continued Dr. Czissar, "was murdered for her money by Arthur and Helen Barrington, who, because they did not want to be found out, arranged alibis for themselves. They were not very useful alibis, because nobody knew exactly when Mrs. Fallon was killed. In my opinion, she was killed between half-past two and twenty-five minutes to three on the afternoon of her disappearance. She was placed in the sea at Haywick Dunes between six and seven o'clock that evening."

"But—"

"The murder," pursued Dr. Czissar firmly, "was very carefully thought out. You remember the drive up to the Grange, Inspector? It is long and winding, Assistant-Commissioner Mercer, and most of it is invisible from the house because of trees.

"At half-past two Barrington left to keep his appointment at Haywick. But instead of driving straight there, he stopped his car a little way down the road and walked back to the drive. Five minutes later his wife left to motor Mrs. Fallon into Seabourne. As soon as she was out of sight of the house, but in the drive, she stopped. Her husband then killed Mrs. Fallon with the weapon he had ready. A coal or mason's hammer would have been suitable. He was a coal and builders' merchant, I think. He then went back to his car and drove on to his appointment at Haywick. Mrs. Barrington also drove on to Seabourne."

"And where, pray, was the body?" inquired Mercer acidly.

"On the floor at the back of Mrs. Barrington's car, with a rug covering it. They could not leave it among the trees, in case it should by chance be discovered. Barrington could not take it in his car. He had appointments to keep, and his car would be left in the road for long periods unattended. In the large municipal car park, Mrs. Barrington's car would be safe from inspection. There is only one attendant, and he is at the gate.

"At half-past five, I think, Mrs. Barrington left the cinema, returned to her car, and drove to the Haywick Dunes, where she had arranged to meet her husband. High tide was at six o'clock. It must have been about then that they arranged to meet. It would be dusk then, too. And that place is very lonely and deserted. The chances of Barrington's being seen as he carried the body to the water were small, I think. No doubt Mrs. Barrington then drove back to Seabourne to make the necessary inquiries of her aunt's friends. That is all, I think."

There was silence for a moment. It was broken by the Inspector.

"I don't see where the furnace comes into it," he remarked.

"The rug and the car mats would be soaked with blood, Inspector. Mrs. Barrington would no doubt put them into the furnace after it had been banked-up for the night. Even such thick materials would be charred and destroyed, but they would put the fire out unless the dampers were also opened. Probably the niece of a rich aunt would not know much about furnaces."

"However," said Mercer sourly, "you have yet, Dr.

Czissar, to explain the presence of the locket on the beach. They might, assuming that this—this theory of yours is correct, have taken the locket from the body. But I refuse to believe that they would, *after* the disappearance of Mrs. Fallon, have risked detection by planting the locket on the beach. The risks would have been enormous, even at night. If he had been caught with it, why—"

"Ah, yes. The locket." Dr. Czissar smiled. "I read about police matters in so many newspapers, you know, that I sometimes forget things I have read, even if they interested me. There is so much crime, is there not? Even in law-abiding England." Was there, Mercer wondered, the faintest note of mockery in the fellow's voice? Confound him!

"It was," said Dr. Czissar, "something I saw the other day in a second-hand jeweller's window that reminded me of the Barringtons."

He put his hand in his pocket. It reappeared holding something that swung from a thin, yellow chain. It was a pinchbeck locket in the shape of a heart.

"The jeweller said," went on Dr. Czissar, "that these things were quite common. Out of date, he said. One can buy such a locket almost anywhere if one tries. Perhaps there was one bought in Seabourne or Haywick recently. It could have been put on the beach on the night before the murder. After all, it was Mrs. Barrington, wasn't it, who identified it as the particular locket that her aunt wore? Clever criminals are so stupid, are they not?"

He looked at his watch. "I suggest also that you find out if Barrington purchased the new car mats and rug before or after the murder, and if anyone saw his wife driving towards Haywick on the fourth. And a detailed account of Barrington's movements after half-past five would, no doubt, provide you with more of the evidence you need for a conviction."

He got suddenly to his feet. "But I must really be going. So kind of you. Enchanted. Enchanted."

Mercer, in a daze, found himself returning once more the stiff little bow and the blank, cow-like stare. Then Dr. Czissar was gone.

"Phew!" said the Inspector loudly. "I thought—"

Mercer pulled himself together. "I'll see you later, Denton," he said sharply. "Sergeant, see if you can find me some aspirin for this cold of mine."

The door closed again and Mercer was alone.

He waited for a moment, staring hopelessly at the untouched pile of work in front of him. Then he drew a deep breath and picked up the telephone.

"I want," he said, "to speak to the Chief Constable of Wessex."

11 / The Case of the Emerald Sky

Assistant-Commissioner Mercer stared without speaking at the card which Sergeant Flecker had placed before him.

There was no address: simply—

DR. JAN CZISSAR
LATE PRAGUE POLICE

It was an inoffensive-looking card. An onlooker, who knew only that Dr. Czissar was a refugee Czech, with a brilliant record of service in the criminal investigation department of the Prague police, would have been surprised at the expression of almost savage dislike that spread slowly over the Assistant-Commissioner's healthy face.

Yet, had the same onlooker known the circumstances of Mercer's first encounter with Dr. Czissar, he would not have been so surprised. Just one week had elapsed since Dr. Czissar had appeared out of the blue with a letter of introduction from the almighty Sir Herbert at the Home Office, and Mercer was still smarting as a result of the meeting. No man, least of all a man in charge of a criminal investigation, likes to be told, even very politely, that he doesn't know his job. When the teller not only tells, but proceeds to prove that he is right, pride is damaged. Mercer's expression can be excused.

Sergeant Flecker had seen and interpreted the expression. Now he spoke. "Out, Sir?"

Mercer looked up sharply. "No, Sergeant. In, but too busy!" he snapped, and got on with his work.

Half an hour later Mercer's telephone rang.

"Sir Herbert to speak to you from the Home Office, Sir," said the male operator.

After a long and, to Mercer, extremely irritating interval, Sir Herbert came through.

"Hello, Mercer, is that you? I say, what's this I hear about your refusing to see Dr. Czissar?"

Mercer jumped, but managed to pull himself together. "I did not refuse to see him, Sir Herbert," he said. "I sent down a message that I was too busy to see him."

Sir Herbert snorted. "Now look here, Mercer. I happen to know that it was Dr. Czissar who spotted those Seabourne murderers for you. Not blaming you personally, of course, and I don't propose to mention the matter to the Commissioner. You can't be right every time. We all know that as an organization there's nothing to touch Scotland Yard. My point is, Mercer, that you fellows ought not to be above learning a thing or two from a foreign expert. We don't want any of this professional jealousy. Of course"—there was a significant little pause—"if you feel that it's a bit irregular, I can have a word with the Commissioner."

If it were possible to speak coherently through

clenched teeth, Mercer would have done so. "There's no question of professional jealousy, Sir Herbert. I was, as Dr. Czissar was informed, busy when he called. If he will write in for an appointment, I shall be pleased to see him."

"Good man," said Sir Herbert cheerfully. "But we don't want any of this red-tape business about writing in. He's in my office now. I'll send him over. He's particularly anxious to have a word with you about this Brock Park case. Good-bye."

Mercer replaced the telephone carefully. He knew that if he had replaced it as he felt like replacing it, the entire instrument would have been smashed. For a moment or two he sat quite still. Then, suddenly, he snatched the telephone up again.

"Inspector Cleat, please." He waited. "Is that you, Cleat? . . . Is the Commissioner in? . . . I see. Well, you might ask him as soon as he comes in if he could spare me a minute or two. It's urgent. Right."

He hung up again, feeling a little better. If Sir Herbert could have words with the Commissioner, so could he. The old man could be a devil, but he wouldn't stand for his subordinates being humiliated, insulted and—yes, that was the word—blackmailed by pettifogging politicians. Meanwhile, however, this precious Dr. Czissar wanted to talk about the Brock Park case. Right! Let him! He wouldn't be able to pull *that* to pieces. It was absolutely watertight. He picked up the file on the case. Yes, absolutely watertight.

Three years previously Thomas Medley, a widower of sixty with two adult children, had married Helena Murlin, a woman of forty-two. The four had since lived together in a large house in the London suburb of Brock Park. Medley, who had amassed a comfortable fortune on the Baltic Exchange, had retired from business shortly before his second marriage and had devoted most of his time since to his hobby, gardening. Helena Murlin was an artist, a landscape painter, and in Brock Park it was whispered that her pictures sold for large sums. She dressed both fashionably and smartly, and was disliked by her neighbors. Harold Medley, the son, aged twenty-five, was a medical student at a London hospital. His sister, Janet, was three years younger, and as dowdy as her stepmother was smart.

In the early October of that year, and as a result of an extra-heavy meal, Thomas Medley had retired to bed with a bilious attack. Such attacks had not been unusual. He had had an enlarged liver and had been normally dyspeptic. His doctor had prescribed in the usual way. On his third day in bed the patient had been considerably better. On the fourth day, however, at about four in the afternoon, he had been seized with violent abdominal pains, persistent vomiting, and severe cramps in the muscles of his legs.

These symptoms had persisted for three days, on the last of which there had been tetanic convulsions. He had died that night. The doctor had certified the death as being due to gastroenteritis. The dead man's estate had amounted to roughly £110,000. Half of it went to his wife. The remainder was divided equally between his two children.

A week after the funeral the police had received an anonymous letter suggesting that Medley had been poisoned. Subsequently they had received two further letters. Information had then reached them that several residents in Brock Park had received similar letters and that the matter was the subject of gossip.

Medley's doctor had been approached later. He had reasserted that the death had been due to gastroenteritis, but confessed that the possibility of the condition having been brought about by the wilful administration of poison had not occurred to him. The body had been exhumed by licence of the Home Secretary and an autopsy performed. No traces of poison had been found in the stomach; but in the liver, kidneys, and spleen a total of 1.751 grains of arsenic had been found.

Inquiries had established that on the day on which the poisoning symptoms had appeared, the deceased had had a small luncheon consisting of breast of chicken, spinach (tinned), and one potato.

The cook had partaken of spinach from the same tin without suffering any ill effects. After his luncheon, Medley had taken a dose of the medicine prescribed for him by the doctor. It had been mixed with water for him by his son, Harold.

Evidence had been obtained from a servant that, a fortnight before the death, Harold had asked his father for £100 to settle a racing debt. He had been refused. Inquiries had revealed that Harold had lied. He had been secretly married for nearly six months, and the money had been needed not to pay racing debts, but for his wife, who was about to have a child.

The case against Harold had been conclusive. He had needed money desperately. He had quarrelled with his father. He had known that he was the heir to a quarter of his father's estate. As a medical student in a hospital, he had been in a position to obtain arsenic. The time at which symptoms of poisoning had appeared had shown that the arsenic must have been administered at about the time the medicine had been taken. It had been the first occasion on which Harold had prepared his father's medicine.

The coroner's jury had boggled at indicting him in their verdict, but he had later been arrested and was now on remand.

Mercer sat back in his chair. A watertight case. Sentences began to form in his mind. "This Dr. Czissar, Sir Charles, is merely a time-wasting crank. He's a refugee, and his sufferings have probably unhinged him a little. If you could put the matter to Sir Herbert . . ."

And then, for the second time that afternoon, Dr. Czissar was announced.

Mercer, as it will have been noted, was an angry man that afternoon. Yet, as Dr. Czissar came into the room, he became conscious of a curious feeling of friendliness towards him. It was not entirely the friendliness that one feels towards an enemy one is about to destroy. In his mind's eye he had been picturing Dr. Czissar as an ogre. Now Mercer saw that, with his cow-like eyes behind their thick pebble spectacles, his round, pale face, his drab gray raincoat, and his unfurled umbrella, Dr. Czissar was, after all, merely pathetic. When, just inside the door, Dr. Czissar stopped, clapped his umbrella to his side as if it were a rifle, and said loudly: "Dr. Jan Czissar. Late Prague police. At your service," Mercer very nearly smiled.

Instead he said: "Sit down, Doctor. I'm sorry I was too busy to see you earlier."

"It is so good of you—" began Dr. Czissar earnestly.

"Not at all, Doctor. You, want, I hear, to compliment us on our handling of the Brock Park case."

Dr. Czissar blinked. "Oh, no, Assistant-Commissioner

Mercer," he said anxiously. "I should like to compliment, but it is too early, I think. I do not wish to seem impolite, but . . ."

Mercer smiled complacently. "Oh, we shall convict our man all right, Doctor. I don't think you need worry."

"Oh, but I do worry. You see—he is not guilty."

Mercer hoped that the smile with which he greeted the statement did not reveal his secret exultation. He said blandly, "Are you aware, Doctor, of all the evidence?"

"I attended the inquest," said Dr. Czissar mournfully. "But there will be more evidence from the hospital, no doubt. This Mr. Harold could have stolen enough arsenic to poison a regiment without the loss being discovered."

The fact that the words had been taken out of his mouth disconcerted Mercer only slightly. He nodded.

A faint, thin smile stretched the Doctor's full lips. He settled his glasses on his nose. Then he cleared his throat, swallowed hard, and leaned forward. "Attention, please!" he said sharply.

For some reason that he could not fathom, Mercer felt his self-confidence ooze suddenly away. He had seen that same series of actions, ending with the peremptory demand for attention, performed once before, and it had been the prelude to disaster, to humiliation, to . . . He pulled himself up sharply. The Brock Park case was watertight.

"I'm listening," he said irritably.

"Good." Dr. Czissar wagged one solemn finger. "According to the medical evidence given at the inquest, arsenic was found in the liver, kidneys, and spleen. No?"

Mercer nodded firmly. "1.751 grains. That shows that much more than a fatal dose had been administered. Much more."

Dr. Czissar's eyes gleamed. "Ah, yes. Much more. It is odd, is it not, that so much was found in the kidneys?"

"Nothing odd at all about it."

"Let us leave the point for the moment. Is it not true, Assistant-Commissioner Mercer, that all post-mortem tests for arsenic are for arsenic itself and not for any particular arsenic salt?"

Mercer frowned. "Yes, but it's unimportant. All arsenic salts are deadly poisons. Besides, when arsenic is absorbed by the human body, it turns to the sulphide. I don't see what you're driving at, Doctor."

"My point is, Assistant-Commissioner, that usually it is impossible to tell from a delayed autopsy which form of arsenic was used to poison the body. You agree? It might be arsenious oxide or one of the arsenates or arsenites; copper arsenite, for instance; or it might be a chloride or it might be an organic compound of arsenic. No?"

"Precisely."

"But," continued Dr. Czissar, "what sort of arsenic should we expect to find in a hospital, eh?"

Mercer pursed his lips. "I see no harm in telling you, Doctor, that Harold Medley could easily have secured supplies of either salvarsan or neosalvarsan. They are both important drugs."

"Ehrlich's 606 and 914! Yes, indeed!" said Dr. Czissar. He stared at the ceiling. "Have you seen any of Helena Murlin's paintings, Assistant-Commissioner?"

The sudden change of subject took Mercer unawares. He hesitated. Then: "Oh, you mean Mrs. Medley. No, I haven't seen any of her paintings."

"Such a *chic*, attractive woman," said Dr. Czissar. "After I had seen her at the inquest I could not help wishing to see some of her work. I found some in a gallery near Bond Street." He sighed. "I had expected something clever, but I was disappointed. She is one of those who paint what they think instead of what is."

"Really? I'm afraid, Doctor, that I must—"

"I felt," persisted Dr. Czissar, bringing his cow-like eyes once more to the level of Mercer's, "that the thoughts of a woman who thinks of a field as blue and of a sky as emerald green must be a little strange."

"Modern stuff, eh?" said Mercer. "And now, Doctor, if you've finished, I'll ask you to excuse me. I—"

"Oh, but I have not finished yet," said Dr. Czissar kindly. "I think, Assistant-Commissioner, that a woman who paints a landscape with a green sky is not only strange but also interesting, don't you? I asked the gentlemen at the gallery about her. She produces only a few pictures—about six a year. She earns, perhaps, £100 a year from her work. It is wonderful how expensively she dresses on that sum."

"She had a rich husband."

"Oh, yes. A curious household, don't you think? The daughter Janet is especially curious. I was so sorry that she was so much upset by the evidence at the inquest."

"A young woman probably would be upset at the idea of her brother's being a murderer," said Mercer drily.

"But to accuse herself so violently of the murder."

"Hysteria. You get a lot of it in murder cases." Mercer stood up and held out his hand. "Well,

Doctor, I'm sorry you haven't been able to upset our case this time. If you'll leave your address with the Sergeant as you go, I'll see that you get a pass for the trial," he added with relish.

But Dr. Czissar did not move. "You are going to try this young man for murder, then?" he said slowly. "You have not understood that at which I have been hinting?"

Mercer grinned. "We've got something better than hints, Doctor—a first-class circumstantial case against young Medley. Motive, time and method of administration, source of the poison. Concrete evidence, Doctor! Juries like it. If you can produce one scrap of evidence to show that we've got the wrong man, I'll be glad to hear it."

Dr. Czissar's back straightened and his cow-like eyes flashed. "I do not like your condescension, Assistant-Commissioner!" he said sharply. "I, too, am busy. I am engaged on a work on medical jurisprudence. I desire only to see justice done. I do not believe that, on the evidence you have, you can convict this young man under English law; but the fact of his being brought to trial could damage his career as a doctor. Furthermore, there is the real murderer to be considered. Therefore, in a spirit of friendliness, I have come to you instead of going to Harold Medley's legal advisers. I will now give you your evidence."

Mercer sat down again. He was very angry.

"Attention, please," said Dr. Czissar. He raised a finger. "Arsenic was found in the dead man's kidneys. It is determined that Harold Medley could have poisoned his father with either salvarsan or neosalvarsan. There is a contradiction there. Most inorganic salts of arsenic—white arsenic, for instance—are practically insoluble in water, and if a quantity of such a salt had been administered, we might expect to find traces of it in the kidneys. Salvarsan and neosalvarsan, however, are trivalent organic compounds of arsenic, and are very soluble in water. If either of them had been administered through the mouth, we should not expect to find arsenic in the kidneys."

He paused; but Mercer was silent.

"In what form, therefore, was the arsenic administered?" he went on. "The tests do not tell us, for they detect only the presence of the element, arsenic. That arsenic will also by that time be present as a sulphide. Let us look among the inorganic salts. There is white arsenic; that is arsenious oxide. It is used for dipping sheep. We should not expect to find it in Brock Park. But Mr. Medley was a gardener. What about sodium arsenite, the weed-killer? We heard at the inquest that the weed-killer in the garden was of the kind harmful only to weeds. We come to copper arsenite. Mr. Medley was, in my opinion, poisoned by a large dose of copper arsenite."

"And on what evidence," demanded Mercer, "do you base that opinion?"

"There is, or there has been, copper arsenite in the Medleys' house." Dr. Czissar looked at the ceiling. "On the day of the inquest, Assistant-Commissioner, Mrs. Medley wore a fur coat. I have since found another fur coat like it. The price of the coat was 400 guineas. Inquiries in Brock Park have told me that this lady's husband, besides being a rich man, was also a very mean and unpleasant man. At the inquest his son told us that he had kept his marriage a secret because he was afraid that his father would stop his allowance or prevent his continuing his studies in medicine.

Helena Murlin had expensive tastes. She had married this man so that she could indulge them. He had failed her. That coat she wore, Assistant-Commissioner, was unpaid for. You will find, I think, that she had other debts and that a threat had been made by one of the creditors to approach her husband. She was tired of this man, so much older than she was. Perhaps she had a young lover with no money to spend on her. But you will find these things out. She poisoned her husband. There is no doubt."

"Nonsense!" snarled Mercer. "Of course, we know that she was in debt. But lots of women are. It doesn't make them murderers."

Dr. Czissar smiled gently. "It was the spinach which the dead man had for luncheon before the symptoms of poisoning began that interested me," he said. "Why give spinach when it is out of season? Tinned vegetables are not usually given to an invalid with gastric trouble. And then, when I saw Mrs. Medley's paintings, I understood. The emerald sky, Assistant-Commissioner. It was a fine, rich emerald green, that sky—the sort of emerald green that the artist gets when there is aceto-arsenite of copper in the paint. The firm which supplies Mrs. Medley with her working materials will be able to tell you when she bought it. I suggest, too, that you take the picture—it is in the Summons Gallery—and remove a little of the sky for analysis. As to the administration, you will find that the spinach was prepared at her suggestion and taken to her husband's bedroom by her. Spinach is green and slightly bitter in taste. So is copper arsenite." He sighed. "If there had not been anonymous letters—"

"Ah!" interrupted Mercer. "The anonymous letters! Perhaps you know—"

"Oh, yes," said Dr. Czissar simply. "The daughter, Janet, wrote them. Poor child! She disliked her smart stepmother, and wrote them out of spite. Imagine her feelings when she found that she had—how do you say?—put a noose about her brother's throat. It would be natural for her to try to take the blame herself. Good afternoon, and thank you," he said.

"Good afternoon," said Mercer wearily. The telephone rang.

"The Commissioner to speak to you, Sir," said the operator.

"All right. Hullo. . . . Hullo, Sir Charles. Yes, I did want to speak to you urgently. It was"—he hesitated—"it was about the Brock Park case. I think that we shall have to release young Medley. I've got hold of some new medical evidence that—All right, Sir Charles, I'll come immediately."

III / The Case of the Cycling Chauffeur

It was generally felt by his subordinates at Scotland Yard that the best time to see Assistant-Commissioner Mercer was while he was drinking his afternoon tea. It was at teatime, therefore, that Detective-Inspector Denton took care to present a verbal report on the Mortons Hind case.

The village of Mortons Hind, Denton reported, was five miles from the market town of Penborough. Near the corner of the Penborough and Leicester roads, and about half a mile from the village, stood Mortons Grange, now the home of Mr. Maurice Wretford, a retired City man, and his wife.

At half-past three in the afternoon of November 10, Mr. Wretford's chauffeur, Alfred Gregory, forty, had left the Grange to drive his employer's car to a Penborough garage, which was to hammer out and repaint a buckled wing. The job could not have been finished that day, and Gregory had taken his bicycle with him in the back of the car so that he could ride home. He had never returned to the Grange. At half-past five that evening a motorist driving along a deserted stretch of road about a mile from the Grange had seen the bicycle lying in a ditch, and stopped. A few yards away, also in the ditch and dead, had been Gregory. He had a bullet in his head.

The lead bullet, which was of .22 calibre, had entered the left temple, leaving a small, circular wound halfway between the ear and the eye, torn through the brain tissue, and come to rest within half an inch of the upper surface of the left brain and immediately over the shattered sphenoid. There had been two small fractures of the skull extending from the puncture in the temporal bone, but no sign of scorching or powder-marks. This, and the fact that the diameter of the wound had been less than the diameter of the bullet, had suggested that the shot had been fired at a distance of over six feet from the dead man's head.

The news of the shooting had spread quickly round the village, and late that night a gamekeeper, Harry Rudder, fifty-two, had reported to the police that that same afternoon he had seen a nineteen-year-old youth, Thomas Wilder, shooting at birds with a rook rifle not far from the spot where Gregory's body had been found. Wilder had admitted that he had been firing the rifle the previous day, but denied that he had been near the Penborough road. His rifle had been examined and found to be of .22 calibre.

It had not been until later that day that the post-mortem findings given above had been made known to the police. The fatal bullet had been handed to them at the same time. To their disgust, it had been badly distorted by its impact against the bones of the head. Any identification of rifling-marks had thus been rendered impossible. The bullet might have been fired from any .22 calibre weapon. Nevertheless, there had been a circumstantial case of manslaughter against Wilder to be considered. The Chief Constable of the County had decided to enlist the help of the ballistics experts of Scotland Yard.

The coroner had sat with a jury at the inquest. Gregory had had no living relatives. His employer, Mr. Wretford, had given woebegone evidence of identification. The ballistics expert, Sergeant Blundell, had later given evidence. The bullet had been fired some distance from the deceased and at a level slightly below that of his head. The witness had agreed that a shot, fired from a rifle held to the shoulder of a man six feet in height (Wilder's height was six feet) standing in the meadow to the left of the road, at a bird in the tree on the opposite side of the road, could hit a passing cyclist in the head. The jury returned a verdict of "Accidental death caused by the criminal negligence of Thomas Wilder." Young Wilder had been arrested.

Mercer stirred his second cup of tea rather irritably. "Yes, yes. All quite straightforward, isn't it? It's Blundell's show now. Send in your report in the usual way."

"Yes, Sir—that is to say . . ." And then, to Mercer's amazement, Denton began to blush. "It's straightforward all right, Sir. But"—he hesitated—"but all the same . . ."

"All the same, what?" demanded Mercer.

Denton drew a deep breath. Then: "All the same, Sir, I don't think Wilder's guilty, Sir," he said.

Mercer's frown deepened. "You don't, eh? Why? Come on, Denton, I haven't got all day to waste."

Denton squirmed on his chair. "Well, Sir, it isn't really my idea at all. It was that Czech refugee who was in the Prague police, that Dr. Czissar."

"Who did you say?" asked Mercer ominously.

Denton recognized the tone of voice and blundered on hurriedly. "Dr. Czissar, Sir. He was at the inquest. He spoke to me afterwards and, seeing that he was a friend of Sir Herbert at the Home Office, I thought I'd better humor him. He . . ."

But Mercer was scarcely listening. He was seeing a vision: a vision of a plump, pale man with pebble glasses and cow-like brown eyes, of a man wearing a long gray raincoat and a soft hat too large for him, and carrying an unfurled umbrella; of this same man sitting on the chair now occupied by Denton and politely telling him, Mercer, how to do his job. Twice it had happened. Twice had Dr. Czissar proved that he was right and that Scotland Yard was wrong. And now . . .

Mercer pulled himself together. "All right, Denton. I know Dr. Czissar. Get on."

Denton drew another breath. "Well, Sir, he oozed up to me after the inquest and asked me to give you his compliments. Then he asked me what I thought about the verdict."

"And what did you think?"

"I didn't get a chance to say, Sir. He didn't wait for an answer. He just said, 'Attention, please!' in that way of his and said that Wilder was innocent. All very polite, you know, Sir, but pretty straight."

Mercer did know. Dr. Czissar's politeness set his teeth on edge. "I see. And did he tell you what the proof was, or did you discover it for yourself?"

"Neither, Sir."

"But you said that you believe that Wilder is innocent."

"I do, Sir." Denton hesitated for a moment. "It's that Dr. Czissar, Sir. He gets under your skin. I don't mind saying that, after he'd spoken to me, I took Blundell back with me to have another look at the place where Gregory was found; but I couldn't see anything wrong and neither could Blundell. The hedge varies in height, and there's a bit of a dip in it just there. From the meadow you couldn't see a man on a bike coming until he was right on top of you. The tree's just opposite that dip in the hedge, too. It's a big elm and there's not another tree either side of it for a hundred yards. The whole thing looked as clear as daylight to me: the sort of accident that's bound to happen if you let lads of nineteen play about with guns. And yet . . ."

Mercer smiled dryly. "I should forget Dr. Czissar's little fancies if I were you, Denton. You must remember that he's a refugee. His experiences have probably unhinged him a little. Understandable, of course."

"You mean he's dotty, Sir?" Denton considered the proposition. "Well, he does look it a bit. But, begging your pardon, Sir, he wasn't so dotty about that Seabourne business. And there was that Brock Park case, too. If it hadn't been for him . . . You see, Sir, it's sort of worried me, him going on about Wilder being innocent." He hesitated. "He says he's coming in to see you this afternoon, Sir," he concluded.

"Oh, does he!"

"Yes, Sir. About five." Denton looked anxious. "If you can let me know what he says, Sir, I'd be grateful."

"All right, Denton. I'll let you know."

Denton went out with the buoyant step and the revolting smile of one who realizes that he has handled a difficult situation with tact and resource. Mercer stared after him.

So, he reflected, it had come to this. His subordinates were hanging on the words of this precious Dr. Czissar like—he cast about wildly for a simile—like schoolboys round a Test cricketer. It was worse than humiliating. It was demoralizing. Here was he, Assistant-Commissioner Mercer, sitting in his room waiting for an unemployed Czech policeman to teach him his job. Something would have to be done. But what? To refuse to see the man would be simply to invite trouble with that old fool at the Home Office. Besides—he wrung the confession from his subconscious mind with masochistic savagery—he *wanted* to see Dr. Czissar, and not entirely in the hope of hearing the Czech make a fool of himself. He was—he admitted it bitterly—curious.

He was still staring helplessly at his untasted second cup of tea when Dr. Czissar was announced.

Dr. Czissar came into the room, clapped his umbrella to his side, clicked his heels, bowed and said: "Dr. Jan Czissar. Late Prague police. At your service."

Mercer watched this all too familiar performance with unconcealed dislike. "Sit down, Doctor," he said shortly. "Inspector Denton tells me that you wish to make a suggestion about the Mortons Hind case."

Dr. Czissar sat down carefully and leaned forward. "Thank you, Assistant-Commissioner," he said earnestly. "It is so good of you to receive me again."

Mercer strove to detect the note of mockery which he felt might be there. "No trouble," he returned gruffly.

Dr. Czissar shook his head. "You are so kind. Everyone is so kind. You see, Assistant-Commissioner, the thing which an exile misses most is his work. To me, police work is my life. I am grateful to you for the opportunities which you have given me, an intruder, to make myself of use again."

"Very nice of you to put it that way," Mercer said curtly. "And now, if you've got something to tell me . . ."

Dr. Czissar sat back quickly. Mercer could almost feel his disappointment. "Of course, Assistant-Commissioner," he said stiffly. "I will not waste your time. If it had not been for the innocence of this boy Wilder, I would not have troubled you."

Mercer cleared his throat. "To me, the case seems perfectly straightforward. Our expert, Blundell . . ."

"Ah!" Dr. Czissar's eyes gleamed. "That is the word. Expert. The witness which the lawyers always attack, eh?"

Mercer gave him a wry smile. "Our expert witnesses, Doctor, are practically lawyers themselves. They're used to cross-examination."

"Precisely. Sergeant Blundell was obviously experienced. He answered honestly and sincerely just those questions which were put to him, *as* they were put to him. No more, no less. It is praiseworthy. Unfortunately, such testimony may be misleading."

"What do you mean?"

"Sergeant Blundell was asked, Assistant-Commissioner, whether a shot fired from a rifle held to the shoulder of a man in the field to the left of the road at a bird in the tree on the right of the road could hit a passing cyclist and make a wound such as that found in Mr. Gregory. He very properly answered that it could."

"Well?"

Dr. Czissar smiled faintly. "Sergeant Blundell had taken measurements and made calculations. They were accurate. But he did not actually fire at any bird in that tree himself. His observations were therefore incomplete. His answer was legally correct. Mr. Gregory *could* have been so killed. But he was *not* so killed. And for a simple reason. For Wilder to have fired the shot at that particular angle, the bird would have had to have been on a branch about eighteen feet from the ground. The lowest branch on that tree, Assistant-Commissioner, is about ten feet above that."

Mercer sat up. "Are you sure of that, Doctor?"

"I could not make a mistake about such a thing," said Dr. Czissar with dignity.

"No, no, of course not. Excuse me a moment, Doctor." Mercer picked up the telephone. "I want Inspector Denton and Sergeant Blundell to see me immediately."

There was an embarrassed silence until they came. Then Dr. Czissar was asked to repeat his statement. Denton snapped his fingers.

Mercer looked at Blundell. "Well?"

Blundell reddened. "It's possible, Sir. I can't say that I looked at the thing from that standpoint. Perhaps it was something on the trunk of the tree—a squirrel, perhaps."

Denton grinned. "I can answer that one, Sir. I was brought up in the country. You wouldn't find a squirrel climbing up the trunk of an odd elm-tree by the side of a main road in November. That makes it murder, eh, Doctor?"

Dr. Czissar frowned. "That," he said stiffly, "is for the Assistant-Commissioner to decide, Inspector." He turned courteously to Mercer. "If you will permit me, Assistant-Commissioner, to make a further suggestion?"

Mercer nodded wearily. "Go ahead, Doctor."

A thin smile stretched the Doctor's full lips. He settled his glasses on his nose. Then he cleared his throat, swallowed hard, and leaned forward. "Attention, please," he said sharply.

He had their attention.

"To you, Assistant-Commissioner Mercer," began Dr. Czissar, "I would say that no blame in this matter belongs to Inspector Denton or Sergeant Blundell. They were obviously expected by the local police to prove a case of manslaughter against Wilder, and they contrived to do so. The case was spoilt for them before they arrived. This man Gregory was found shot. Either he was shot accidentally or he was murdered. A small community dislikes the thought of murder even more than a large one. But they do not have to think of murder, for here, under their noses, is a better explanation. Wilder was firing a .22 rifle. Gregory was killed with a .22 bullet. *Ergo*, Wilder killed Gregory. Everyone is happy—except Wilder and myself. I am not happy; especially when I see that the shooting could not have happened as is said. It seems to me that even though the local police dislike the idea, murder has been done. Who has done it? I begin, logically, with the victim."

"At the inquest," resumed Dr. Czissar, "Mr. Wretford, so sad at losing his good chauffeur, said that Gregory had been in his employ for three years, and that he was sober, steady, and of excellent character. And the poor man had no friends or relations living. Such a pity, and so unusual. I decided to investigate a little. I went to the garage at Penborough and talked to a mechanic there. I found that Mr. Wretford had made a little mistake about his chauffeur. Gregory was not very sober. Also, he betted a great deal for a man in his position. The mechanic was able to tell me that he dealt with a bookmaker in Penborough. To this bookmaker I went."

Dr. Czissar looked suddenly embarrassed. "I am afraid," he said apologetically, "that I have been guilty of an offense. You see, Assistant-Commissioner Mercer, I wished for information from this bookmaker. I said that I was from the police, without saying that it was the Prague police. I found that Gregory had, in the last twelve months, lost two hundred and thirty-seven pounds to this bookmaker."

Mercer jumped. "What!"

"Two hundred and thirty-seven pounds, Assistant-Commissioner. In addition, he had asked for no credit. He had received his winnings and paid his losses in pound notes. His wages, I think, could not have been sufficient to absorb such losses."

"He earned two pounds a week and his keep, according to Wretford," Denton put in.

"Ah, quite so." Dr. Czissar smiled gently. "The bookmaker had concluded that the bets were really made by Mr. Wretford, who did not wish, for personal reasons, to have it known that he betted. It seems that such reticences are not unusual. But Gregory had been murdered. That *was* unusual. The bookmaker's conclusion did not satisfy me. I made other inquiries. Among other things, I found that eight years ago, just before Mr. Wretford retired, a clerk in his office was convicted of stealing the sum of fifteen thousand pounds in bearer bonds and three hundred pounds in cash. I was able to find a full report of the case in the newspaper files. The prosecution showed that he had got into debt through betting and that he had been systematically stealing small sums over a long period. The prosecution argued that, having gained confidence from the fact that his petty thefts went undiscovered, he had stolen the bearer bonds. There was one curious feature about the affair. The bearer bonds were not found and the prisoner refused to say anything about them except that he had stolen them. His sentence was, therefore, unusually severe for a first offender—five years' penal servitude. His name was Selton."

"I remember the case," said Denton eagerly. "Gregory Selton—that was the name."

"Precisely!" said Dr. Czissar. "*Gregory.* A young man who right until his death, was too fond of betting. He must have changed his name when he came out of prison. Now, we find him in the last place we should expect to find him. He is Mr. Wretford's chauffeur. Mr. Wretford, the man he robbed of fifteen thousand pounds!"

Mercer shrugged. "Generous gesture on Wretford's part. It doesn't explain why he was shot or who shot him."

Dr. Czissar smiled. "Nor why Mr. Wretford lied at the inquest?"

"What are you getting at?"

Dr. Czissar held up a finger. "Attention, please! The only logical part of that case against Selton was that he had over a long period stolen sums in cash amounting to three hundred pounds and intended to pay off racing debts. That is the thieving of a clerk. That he should suddenly steal fifteen thousand pounds is absurd. And we only have his word for it that he did steal them."

"But why on earth should . . . ?"

"Mr. Wretford's reputation," pursued Dr. Czissar, "was not very good in the City. I believe that those bonds were converted by Mr. Wretford for his own private profit, and that he was in danger of being found out when he discovered Selton's thefts. He was desperate, perhaps. Selton, he thought, would go to prison, anyway. Let him agree to take a little extra blame and all would be well. Selton would have his reward when he came out of prison. Alas for Mr. Wretford! Mr. Gregory Selton was not content with comfortable and overpaid employment. He began, I think, to blackmail Mr. Wretford. Those racing debts, you see. More money, more money always. Mr. Wretford was very wise to kill him under the circumstances."

"But . . ."

"But, how? Ah, yes." Dr. Czissar smiled kindly upon them. "It was, I think, a sudden idea. The grounds of his house are extensive. He probably heard Wilder using the rook rifle near by and thought of his own rifle. He used to be a member of a City rifle club. Selton would, he knew, be returning soon. It would be possible for him to get from his house to that place behind the hedge without going on to the road and risking being seen. When Selton was found, the blame would be put on this boy. For him, a few months in prison; for the respectable Mr. Wretford, safety. He stood behind the hedge at a range of perhaps ten feet from Selton as he cycled by. It would have been difficult to miss."

Dr. Czissar stood up. "It is a suggestion only, of

course," he said apologetically. "You will be able to identify Selton from his finger-prints and arrest Mr. Wretford on a charge of perjury. The rifle will no doubt be found when you search the Grange. An examination of Mr. Wretford's accounts will show that he was being blackmailed by Selton. Those large sums in one pound notes . . . but it is not for me to teach you your business, eh?" He smiled incredulously at the idea. "It is time for me to go. Good evening, Assistant-Commissioner."

For a moment there was a silence. Then:

"I knew there was something funny about this case, Sir," said Denton brightly. "Clever chaps, these Czechs."

IV / The Case of the Overheated Service Flat

Assistant-Commissioner Mercer did not often attend inquests. It was not part of his duty to do so. The fact that on that foggy December morning he should be sitting in a coroner's court in a London suburb instead of in his room at New Scotland Yard argued wholly exceptional circumstances.

The circumstances were indeed exceptional. It looked as though a murderer were going to escape the consequences of his crime and as if there were nothing that Scotland Yard could do about it.

In 1933 the wife of Mr. Thomas Jones, an industrial chemist living in a Midland town, had died in her bath from carbon-monoxide poisoning. At the inquest her death had been found to be due to a defective geyser. Three months previously Mr. Jones had insured her life for £5000; but although the police reviewed the possibility of his having engineered the defect in the geyser, no proof of his having done so had been forthcoming. A verdict of "Accidental Death" had been returned.

In 1935 Mr. Jones had married again. His second wife had been fifteen years his senior. It had been, no doubt, the £15,000 which the second Mrs. Jones had inherited from her mother that had bridged the difference in their ages. But Mr. Jones was, it seemed, unlucky in love. Eighteen months after their marriage the second Mrs. Jones had died; and, strange to relate, from carbon-monoxide poisoning. She had been found in her car, which had been inside the garage with the engine running. According to the hapless Mr. Jones, his wife had been subject to fainting fits. Evidently she had driven the car into the garage, felt faint, and remained in the driving-seat. There had been a strong wind and no doubt the garage doors had blown to, leaving her at the mercy of the exhaust fumes. The fact that a small quantity of veronal had been found in her stomach had, to the irritation of the police, been accounted for by her doctor, who had said that she had been in the habit of taking sleeping draughts. A verdict of "Accidental Death" had been returned.

In 1938 Mr. Jones, now of independent means, had married yet again. His third wife's name had been Rose, and she had had an income of £1200 a year from freehold house property left to her by her father. The week before the inquest which Mercer was now attending Mrs. Jones had died—from carbon-monoxide poisoning.

The couple had lived in a block of expensive service flats. According to a preternaturally lugubrious Mr. Jones, he had been at his golf club on the afternoon of "the tragedy" and had returned home at about six o'clock to find the flat full of coal-gas and his wife dead in her bed. The gas-fire in the bedroom had been turned full on. His wife, he said, had been of a "sunny" disposition, and he could think of no reason why she should have "taken her life." In his opinion, propounded at length to the police inspector, she had been getting into bed for her afternoon nap, had caught the hem of her house-coat on the tap, and in freeing it had unwittingly turned the tap on. The fumes—here Mr. Jones had exercised visible restraint over his emotions—had overcome her while she had been asleep.

Mercer listened to the evidence gloomily. With the facts about Mr. Jones's earlier matrimonial adventures in mind, Mercer had no doubt that Rose Jones had been murdered. The difficulty was to prove it. The law, very rightly, prohibited any mention of the fate of Mr. Jones's first two wives while the fate of the third was still *sub judice*. No doubt Mr. Jones was aware of that. Mercer saw that the man was making an excellent impression on the jury. A demure figure in deep mourning, he was giving his evidence with sublime disregard of the implications contained in the questions being put to him.

Yes, he had given instructions for the gas-fire to be installed. No, it had been at his wife's request that he had done so. No, it was not strange that she should need a gas-fire in a centrally heated room. She had felt the cold. Yes, it was the only gas-fire in the flat. There was a portable electric radiator in another room, but his wife had not liked it in the bedroom.

No, it was not strange that he had insisted upon an old-type gas-fire instead of the new type with the tap built into the fire. His wife had expressed a preference for the former. He was sorry now that he had not insisted upon the new type. The accident could not then have happened.

He had left his wife at two-thirty to go to his golf club, ten minutes' walk away. No, he had not gone straight there. He had gone first to a newsagent's shop and bought a fashion magazine for his wife. He had then returned to the entrance lobby to the flats and asked the hall porter to take the magazine up to Mrs. Jones. He had then gone on to the golf club.

No, he had not seen his wife alive after leaving the flat at two-thirty. The hall porter must have been the last person to see her alive. As far as he could remember, he had arrived at the golf club at about three o'clock. But he couldn't be certain. The secretary at the golf club would probably remember. He had met him soon after he had arrived.

Yes (this with a puzzled frown), there was a gas-meter in the flat. Yes, the main gas-tap was beside it. As far as he could remember, the meter was at the top of a cupboard just inside the door of the flat. Yes, he believed that he had suggested its installation there instead of in the kitchen. To have installed it in the kitchen would have meant loss of cupboard-space.

The jury, Mercer noted, were beginning to fidget. Clearly they did not see the point of this questioning. He scowled at them. The blockheads! They had been shown a plan of the flats. And didn't they ever read their newspapers? Couldn't they visualize the scene? Mr. Jones turning the gas off at the main and then turning on the gas-fire in the bedroom; Mr. Jones returning to the lobby with a magazine; the hall porter going up in the lift to deliver the magazine while Mr. Jones ascended again by the stairs? Couldn't they see Mr. Jones waiting on the stairs while the hall porter descended again and his wife got into bed? Couldn't they see Mr. Jones quietly opening the door of the flat, reaching up to the cupboard, turning the main gas-tap on again, and quietly leaving? The hall porter had admitted that he didn't watch the entrance all the time. Didn't they see that Mr. Jones could have done these things and got to his golf club in time to show himself to a doddering old fool of a secretary "soon after" three? It must be obvious. "Blockheads!" he muttered, and heard Detective-Inspector Denton beside him stir in sympathy.

And then he saw Dr. Czissar.

The refugee Czech detective was sitting in one of the seats reserved for the Press and as his brown, cow-like eyes met Mercer's gray ones, he inclined his head respectfully.

Mercer nodded curtly and looked away. He heard Denton's grunt of surprise and hoped that his subordinate would not find it necessary to comment on Dr. Czissar's presence at the inquest. The last person he wanted to think about at that moment was Dr. Jan Czissar. Since the first day on which this pale, bespectacled Czech had walked into his office bearing an unfurled umbrella and a letter of introduction from a Home Office politician, Mercer had been nursing a badly wounded self-esteem. Twice had the wound been reopened. Three times in all had he had to listen to Dr. Czissar demonstrating, with his infuriating lecture-room mannerisms, that Scotland Yard could be wrong while he, Dr. Jan Czissar, "late Prague police," was right.

Now, as he sat listening to a gas company official confirming Mr. Jones's account of the installation of the gas-fire, Mercer tried to put Dr. Czissar out of his mind. But his mind, nagged by the memories of past humiliations, refused to part with Dr. Czissar. It began to speculate as to why Dr. Czissar was there at the inquest, what he was doing in the Press seats, and what he was thinking about the case. It was with a heartfelt sigh of relief that he heard the coroner's announcement that the court would adjourn for the luncheon interval.

He stood up. "We might get a drink and a sandwich across the road, Denton."

"Right, Sir."

They had gone about three paces before Nemesis, worming its way between a policeman and a stout member of the general public, overtook them.

"Assistant-Commissioner Mercer, please," said Dr. Czissar breathlessly, "Dr. Jan Czissar. Late Prague police. At your service. I should like, if you please, to speak about this case." He bowed quickly to Denton.

Mercer gave him a rancid smile. "Ah, Dr. Czissar! Are you working for the Press now, Doctor?"

Dr. Czissar hesitated. "The Press? No, I am still working on my book on medical jurisprudence. Ah, I see. The seat. It was lent to me by a journalist with a Press card. But"—he smiled shyly—"perhaps I should not say that, eh?"

Mercer grunted. The Doctor, his long, gray raincoat flapping about his legs, was now loping along beside them. Denton, who, with less dignity to lose than Mercer, thought Dr. Czissar very clever indeed, would have liked to have discussed the case, but seeing Mercer's face, kept silent.

"I was very surprised," pursued Dr. Czissar as they descended the steps to the street, "to see you in this court this morning, Assistant-Commissioner. It appeared such an unimportant case. But then, of course, I had not heard the evidence. I wish to compliment you, Assistant-Commissioner. It was so clever, I thought, the way in which the existence of the electric radiator was established. I was afraid for a time that the murderer's trick was going to succeed. But I should have known better. It is a most interesting case."

But Mercer had stopped dead. "What did you say about an electric radiator?" he demanded.

Dr. Czissar looked a little scared as he repeated the sentence.

"May I remind you, Doctor," snapped Mercer, "that Mrs. Jones was not burnt to death or electrocuted, but gassed?"

A puzzled look came over the Doctor's face. "But I thought," he said hesitantly, "that you understood . . ." He did not finish the sentence. The puzzled look on his face gave way to one of acute embarrassment. He drew himself up. "I beg your pardon, Assistant-Commissioner," he said formally. "I have made a mistake. If you will excuse me, please?"

At that moment something inside Mercer's stomach seemed to drop about six inches, and in the fraction of a second which it took to do so, he realized that his humiliations at the hands of Dr. Czissar were not ended; that the wound was to be opened yet again. There was nothing else for it. Dr. Czissar had obviously understood something about the case that he had not understood. He, Mercer, must know what that something was before the inquest ended in a verdict of "Accidental Death." And there was only one way of finding out. He steeled himself for the ordeal. Then:

"I should very much like to discuss the case with you, Doctor," he said ceremoniously. "Inspector Denton and I were about to take a little refreshment. If you would care to accompany us . . ."

Three minutes later a thoroughly bewildered Dr. Czissar was sitting with a whisky-and-soda and a ham sandwich in front of him. "It is most kind of you, Assistant-Commissioner," he was repeating over and over again. The brown eyes behind the thick pebble glasses were almost tearful.

"Not at all." Mercer took a deep breath. "I have a confession to make to you, Doctor. We do not *know* that this is a case of murder. We only *believe* so. Jones has had three wives, of which this woman was the third. All have died apparently accidental deaths from carbon-monoxide poisoning. All three deaths have been of financial benefit to Jones. That is the basis of our belief that Jones is a murderer. But from the evidence at our disposal we are frankly unable to prove it. In our opinion, as you will have gathered from the questions asked this morning, Jones returned to the flat before he went to the golf club and turned on the main gas-tap so that the gas escaped into his wife's room while she was asleep. All he would have to do before he went out would be to leave the fire tap on and the main tap off. But it is proof we need. Now, Doctor, you've helped us before. If you can help up again we shall be obliged."

Dr. Czissar's pleasure was, Denton thought, pathetic. "Assistant-Commissioner Mercer," he said eagerly, "I am profoundly honored by your confidence. It is a great joy to me to be able to help the nation which has shown such hospitality to me and others of my unhappy countrymen. I, too, will be frank. But for your presence in court I should have stopped to hear no more than the medical evidence. Now I will tell you this. If I had known what you have now told me about Mr. Jones, I do not think that I should have understood this case. He is a very clever man. I will explain to you why."

"Please do," said Mercer drily.

A faint, thin smile stretched the Doctor's full lips. He settled his spectacles on his nose. Then he cleared his throat, swallowed hard, and leaned forward. "Attention, please!" he said sharply.

"In the first place," said Dr. Czissar, "I considered this story of the gas-fire being turned on accidentally. I tried to think of it actually happening. There is a tap, and this lady has a long coat which catches in the tap, turning it on. So far it is possible. Improbable, as are all accidents, but possible. What happens now? According to Mr. Jones's evidence, the tap was turned full on when he returned to the flat and found his wife dead. Therefore we are asked to believe that while the lady was taking off her coat, getting into bed and going to sleep, the tap was all the time turned fully on. That, I thought, was not possible. Assistant-Commissioner, I will explain why."

"We'll accept the proposition," put in Mercer hastily.

"To begin with," persisted Dr. Czissar, "a gas-fire turned full on and unlighted makes a little noise. But let us assume that this lady was a little deaf. There is now the *smell* of the gas to be considered. My own sense of smell is not particularly sensitive, but I can easily detect one part of coal-gas in seven hundred parts of air. Many persons—especially those who do not smoke—can detect by smell one part in ten thousand. Is it credible that this lady should be awake in a small room for several minutes with the gas-fire turned full on without smelling it? I think no!"

"The accident, then, is impossible. And is not the police theory also impossible? Mr. Jones leaves the flat at half-past two. At two-thirty-five he hands the magazine to the hall porter. He then has to go up the stairs and wait until the porter has gone and his wife is asleep. Let us assume that he knows his wife's habits very well and that he can be sure when she will go to sleep. He will have to wait on the stairs at least twenty minutes. Then he has to leave the building and reach the golf club without being seen. The risk to him would have been enormous. He might have been seen on the stairs by one of the other tenants. I cannot believe that a man like Mr. Jones would have taken such a risk."

"Then it wasn't murder?" said Denton.

Dr. Czissar smiled. "Oh, yes, it was murder, Inspector. There is no doubt of it. But consider Mr. Jones's cleverness. He planned to murder his third wife. Very well. He realized at once that however skillfully he made it look like an accident, the police would suspect murder because of the first two cases you mention to me. Here is his cleverness: he decides to use your suspicions to make himself quite safe from conviction. You believed, naturally, that he stole back and turned on the main tap. Think how much he helped you to that belief! He had the gas-fire installed in spite of the fact that there was efficient steam-heating in the room. Very suspicious. He asked specially for an obsolete type of fire, which would enable him to say that the affair was accidental. Very suspicious. His alibi is not perfect. Again suspicious.

The only thing he did not help you to was the *proof* that he returned to the flat. And he knows that you cannot get it for yourselves. Why? Because it does not exist. He did *not* return to the flat. He is therefore safe. What does it matter to him if he is suspect? You cannot prove anything against him, because you are trying to prove something that did not happen."

"Blimey!" said Denton.

"Blind you, indeed!" agreed Dr. Czissar courteously. "For me, however, things were different. I did not know of these other murders. I saw only the facts of this case. I saw only a woman poisoned by carbon-monoxide and a man who has been an industrial chemist inheriting a fortune. Coal-gas? So *he* says. But he is suspect."

"But, dammit—!" began Mercer explosively.

"Coal-gas," pursued Dr. Czissar, "is undoubtedly poisonous because of the carbon-monoxide contained in it. But for an industrial chemist there would be other ways of filling a room with carbon-monoxide. A small charcoal brazier, for instance."

"There was," said Mercer, "no charcoal brazier in the flat."

"Nor any sign of one," added Denton.

Dr. Czissar giggled. "Dear me, no. I did not expect that there was. I give you only an example. But did you notice, Assistant-Commissioner, that although much was made of the strangeness of the gas-fire in a steam-heated flat, no one found it strange that there should also be an electric radiator there."

"You mean he put charcoal on the electric radiator?"

"No, please." Dr. Czissar raised a finger admonishingly. "I did not say that. The man is a chemist. What is the Laboratory method of preparing pure carbon-monoxide? I will tell you. One reduces chalk by heating it with zinc dust. He would not need much. One part of carbon-monoxide in one hundred parts of air is a sufficient concentration to kill in a very short time—little more than an hour. And pure carbon-monoxide has *no* smell."

"But—"

"Attention, please!" said Dr. Czissar sharply. "I think the murder was done this way. Before he went out that day, Mr. Jones took the radiator and put it on its back underneath his wife's bed. He then sprinkled the heater elements all over with the mixture of chalk and zinc dust, and, having plugged the radiator into the power point, said good-bye. Next, he sent the hall porter up with the magazine to establish that his wife was alive when he left. But she was not alive for long. When the radiator became hot, the chalk and zinc dust reacted together and produced large quantities of carbon-monoxide. When he returned home at six o'clock she was dead. He then removed the radiator and turned on the gas-fire. When the flat smelled strongly of coal-gas he summoned help."

"But the proof, man—the proof!"

"Oh, yes. The zinc dust would have to be purchased from a laboratory supplier. It is much used as a reducing agent. Examination of the radiator will be helpful also. Your chemists will be able to find traces of both calcium and zinc oxides on the elements. And it is probable that the carpet under the bed will be scorched. Even the backs of radiators get very hot."

Mercer looked at Denton. "Better ask the coroner for an adjournment, hadn't we, Sir?"

Mercer nodded. Then he looked again at Dr. Czissar, who was nibbling his sandwich.

"Well, Doctor," he said as heartily as he could, "we've got to thank you once again." He raised his glass. "Here's to you!"

Dr. Czissar dropped his sandwich. His pale cheeks flushed slightly. He beamed with pleasure.

"I have not yet tasted English whisky," he said quickly, "but I know the English toast." He raised his glass. "Cheerio! All the best!" he said in ringing tones.

He drank, put the glass down, and shuddered violently.

"All the best," he rejoined bravely, and took a large bite out of the sandwich.

V / The Case of the Drunken Socrates

There are at New Scotland Yard patient, disillusioned men whose business it is to examine the work of England's great army of anonymous letter-writers. They read, they classify, they file. One letter in a thousand may possibly be worth more than momentary consideration. Assistant-Commissioner Mercer can scarcely be blamed for the attitude which he adopted towards the affair which the newspapers later called "the drunken Socrates case."

Yet it must be admitted that, even had there been no question of anonymous letters, Mercer would have disliked the case from the beginning. The reason is simple. The case was brought to his notice by Dr. Jan Czissar.

A wound to his self-esteem is unpleasant enough even for an ordinary man. For an Assistant-Commissioner at Scotland Yard it is positively demoralizing. And when it is considered that Dr. Czissar had inflicted on him not one such wound, but four, Mercer must be excused. On four separate occasions had Dr. Czissar been able to prove, politely but irrefutably, that Scotland Yard in general and Assistant-Commissioner Mercer in particular were not infallible; and, though a simple soul might expect Mercer to be grateful, he was not.

It so happened that on the December afternoon on which Dr. Czissar chose to intrude for the fifth time into the affairs of Scotland Yard, Mercer was feeling pleased with himself. He had just brought a difficult case to a triumphant conclusion. The Commissioner had congratulated him. The very existence of Dr. Czissar had been forgotten. He felt strong and capable.

And then Dr. Czissar was announced.

Wounds to the self-esteem do not heal easily; not even when they are forgotten. If Mercer was surprised and annoyed by the sudden tightening inside his chest which was the immediate result of the announcement, he was infuriated by the behavior of his mind. Before he realized it, his mind was passing in quick review the various cases on which his department was working at the moment and wondering which of them was about to receive the disruptive attention of Dr. Czissar. He pulled himself together savagely. He was losing his sense of proportion.

"All right," he said wearily. "I'll see him."

A minute later he heard the flapping of Dr. Czissar's long drab raincoat echoing along the corridor outside and waited, like a prisoner awaiting the next turn of the thumb-screw, for Dr. Czissar's inevitable greeting. It came. The Doctor walked into the room, halted, clapped his unfurled umbrella to his side, clicked his heels, and intoned loudly: "Dr. Jan Czissar. Late Prague police. At your service!"

"How are you, Doctor? Please take a seat."

The round, pale face relaxed. The brown, cow-like eyes enlarged behind the thick pebble spectacles.

"I am well, thank you, Assistant-Commissioner Mercer." He sat down. "Quite well, but a little worried. Otherwise I would not take your time. It is about a very curious case."

Mercer steeled himself. "Yes?" He laughed with ghastly jocularity. "What has the Yard done this time, Doctor? Let another murderer slip through its fingers?"

Dr. Czissar looked shocked. "Oh, no, please. I think that that is most unlikely. Everything is most efficient here. There is, I think, a murder to be considered but I do not think that Scotland Yard has failed. The police do not know of this case. I must explain that it is only because of my landlady that I know of it."

"Your landlady?"

"I live, Assistant-Commissioner, in Metternich Square, in Bloomsbury. It is a very nice house. Very clean, and there are only four other lodgers—students at the University. It is owned by my landlady, Mrs. Falcon. It is this lady who, knowing that I have some experience in police matters, brought the matter to me for my advice." The cow-like eyes became more pathetic. "And so now, Assistant-Commissioner Mercer, I bring it to *you* for advice, if you will be so kind."

Advice! Dr. Czissar was asking *him* for advice! Mercer could scarcely believe his ears.

"Of course, Doctor. Anything we can do."

"You are so kind. May I tell you about this case?"

"Yes. Please do."

"It begins," said Dr. Czissar solemnly, "with a

death. On June 20 of this year my landlady's brother, Captain Pewsey, died suddenly at his house in Meresham, which is a town twenty miles from London. It was a very distressing thing for my landlady, who was very fond of her brother, in spite of his faults. You see, Assistant-Commissioner, he drank too much whisky. About five years ago he married a woman much younger than he was. Mrs. Falcon thinks that this Mrs. Pewsey did not make him happy.

"I have said that the Captain drank a lot. About a week before his death he went to a doctor in Meresham and complained of his heart. The doctor examined him and found a little cardiac weakness. He advised the Captain to drink less whisky and to live carefully. There was no great danger, he said, but it would be as well if the Captain avoided excesses.

"For several days after that visit to the doctor the Captain drank less whisky, but on the night of June 20 he spent the evening with a friend—Mr. Stenson.

"The Captain was in the business of selling life insurance policies, and he had met Mr. Stenson through selling him a policy. The friendship continued through the game of golf. There was, perhaps, a financial reason for the Captain's liking for Mr. Stenson: Mr. Stenson works in the City of London and he has made much money and knows important persons. The Captain would have found him useful.

"The first part of that evening of the 20th the Captain spent with Mr. Stenson and other men at the golf club; but at about ten o'clock the Captain and Mr. Stenson left the club together and walked towards their houses. Mr. Stenson's house was reached first and the Captain went in with him to drink more whisky. Soon after eleven o'clock the Captain left and went to his own house. It seems that he was then a little drunk. His wife had already gone to bed, and she said afterwards that she heard him stumble along the passage to his room. Then she went to sleep. In the morning, when she went into his room, she found him sitting in an armchair still dressed. He was very blue in the face and seemed dead.

"She called the doctor immediately. He came and found that the Captain was indeed dead. The doctor was a little puzzled. He had examined the Captain a week before, but he had not thought that his heart was in so bad a state that a little too much whisky would kill him. He told these things to Mrs. Pewsey and said that before signing the death certificate he would ask her permission to make a post-mortem examination. She was reluctant, but as he insisted, she agreed. He made the examination, found that the death had been due to a respiratory failure, and concluding that the cause of it had been the weakness of the heart, issued a certificate to that effect."

"A very cautious doctor," commented Mercer.

Dr. Czissar's cow-like eyes contemplated his. "Doctors should always be cautious, I think. But I will continue with the story. A month ago Mr. Stenson married Mrs. Pewsey."

Mercer raised his eyebrows. "Quick work!"

Dr. Czissar nodded sadly. "That is what Mrs. Falcon thought. She heard about the marriage from a friend who lives at Meresham. She was most upset. She had rarely seen her brother since his marriage, as she did not like Mrs. Pewsey; but her affection for him remained. She thought it unpleasant that his widow should have shown so little respect for his memory. It was also a surprise to her, for she had heard nothing of any friendship between the two at the funeral. And then"—he delved into his pocket and produced three folded sheets of notepaper—"Mrs. Falcon showed these to me. There are three of them, and they are marked in order."

Mercer took the sheets and selected Number One.

> "DEAR MRS. FALCON [he read]—
>
> *"Your sister-in-law has married your brother's friend. So soon! Strange, is it not? I should ask a few questions if I were you. Why did your brother die? He was in the prime of life. He had the best years before him. Doctors don't know everything. Captain Pewsey was as strong as an ox.—Yours truly,* A FRIEND."

It was typewritten. He glanced quickly at the remaining letters, saw that they were similar and looked up.

"Well, Doctor? We get plenty of this sort of thing here. Do you know who wrote them?"

Dr. Czissar nodded. "Oh, yes. Mrs. Falcon wrote them."

"To herself!"

"Yes. She said that she had thrown the envelopes away. Also"—Dr. Czissar smiled sadly—"there are phrases there of which Mrs. Falcon is very fond. Mrs. Falcon is a kind woman, but she is disappointed. She had hoped, I think, that her brother, the Captain, would leave her some money. But those letters are interesting, are they not?"

"The usual poisonous trash."

"Oh, yes. But interesting. They succeeded in their

object too. Mrs. Falcon wished me to go down to Meresham and make a scandal with questions. I have been and I have asked some questions. There will also, I think, be a scandal."

"But you surely don't take this stuff seriously?"

"I do." Dr. Czissar leaned forward. "And I wish you to do so also, Assistant-Commissioner."

"But why? The suggestion is, I suppose, that Stenson killed Pewsey. From the facts you have given me, that's obviously absurd. Pewsey was a heavy drinker with a weak heart. He got drunk, had a heart attack and died. The cause of death is confirmed by an autopsy. Perfectly straightforward. If your Mrs. Falcon isn't careful, she'll find these accusations of hers landing her in the dock."

The sad brown eyes blinked. "But, Assistant-Commissioner, Mrs. Falcon makes no accusations. Nor do I think that she believes that there is anything seriously wrong. She wishes only, as I have said, to make a scandal, to revenge herself on her sister-in-law. She comes to me principally for sympathy and because she wishes to talk about the affair. She is very satisfied that I have been to Meresham, but when I returned she even forgot to ask me about the possibility of her brother's death being unnatural. The suggestion in these letters was purely malicious. She had no idea that it was a sound suggestion. No, Assistant-Commissioner, it is not Mrs. Falcon but I who make the accusation."

Mercer sat back. "And who are you accusing, Doctor?"

Dr. Czissar cleared his throat and swallowed hard. "Attention, please!" he said sharply.

"I am all attention," snapped Mercer.

"Good. Then I will begin by giving you the facts. The first is contained in Mrs. Falcon's letters to herself. Three months after the Captain's death, Mrs. Pewsey marries Mr. Stenson. 'So soon! Strange, is it not?' says Mrs. Falcon. It is indeed strange, Assistant-Commissioner. Three months is a very short time in which to bury one husband, adjust one's mind to the idea of widowhood, adjust one's mind again to the idea of replacing the dead husband with a new one, and then marry him. One might reach a decision in so short a time, but actually to marry as well. . . . It is, I think, unreal. It seems to me as if the idea of the marriage had been in the minds of Mrs. Pewsey and Mr. Stenson *before* the Captain died."

"You can't prove that, Doctor," said Mercer quickly.

"There is corroborative evidence, Assistant-Commissioner. In the first place, there is the matter of their secrecy. It is not easy, I should think, to keep a secret in a small town like Meresham. Yet, had a member of the Meresham Golf Club not encountered Mr. Stenson and the lady in a London hotel the day after they were married, no one in Meresham would even have known that the two had even spoken to one another. Yet, if all was well, they had no reason for secrecy. As the Captain's friend, Mr. Stenson would have had a perfectly good reason for seeing Mrs. Pewsey in Meresham. But, and I have the authority of Mrs. Pewsey's maid for the statement, Stenson had only once been in the Pewsey's house. He had had dinner there one evening a year or more before the Captain died. Secrecy becomes a habit, Assistant-Commissioner. There was secrecy after the Captain's death because there had been need for secrecy before it.

"Another point. There was, I discovered, a great difference between the characters of Mr. Stenson and the Captain. Mr. Stenson was very popular. He had money. He played golf well. He was noted for his sense of humor. He was handsome. The Captain, however, was most unpopular. He was always trying to do business with people. He drank too much. He played golf badly. He was a bore. Nobody in Meresham could understand why Mr. Stenson put up with him. That he did so is most significant."

Mercer pursed his lips. "If you don't mind my saying so, Doctor, I think you've let yourself read more into this business than is really there."

The cow-like eyes grew rounder and sadder. "Yes? I will continue. I have interviewed Mrs. Pewsey's maid. The house is shut up at the moment, but she was there on the night that the Captain died. Her evidence is interesting—vitally interesting, I think. She heard the Captain return home to die.

"She says that she had never known him so drunk before. He fell up the stairs and stumbled along the passage to his bedroom. And he was talking to himself. He had never done that before. As he passed the door to her room, she heard one sentence clearly. He was mumbling and then he said: 'Socrates! What's he mean, Socrates? My name's not Socrates.' She heard no more. But she heard enough, I think."

Mercer threw up his hands. "I'm sorry, Doctor. I just don't understand. The man was very drunk. Not an unnatural thing in a heavy drinker. Remember, too, that he had been drinking less since he had seen the doctor a week before. He had broken out again. It overstrained his heart. He died. The doctor's autopsy proves it beyond doubt."

"You think that?" Dr. Czissar looked mournful. "The cause of death was a respiratory failure."

"Precisely. Loss of breath. Most of us die from it sooner or later." Mercer stood up. The spell was broken. Dr. Czissar was, after all, merely a crank. By freakish chance he had managed to succeed in one or two cases in which the Yard had looked like failing. Now, he had shown himself up. Mercer smiled tolerantly.

"Doctor," he said, "you asked me for my advice in this business. I will give it to you. Go back to your landlady and tell her not to be stupid. And forget about the matter yourself. That is all, I think." He held out his hand.

But Dr. Czissar did not rise to take it.

"This, as I have said, is a case of murder, Assistant-Commissioner," he said deliberately. "Justice must be done. I have given you the facts. I ask you only to draw conclusions."

"I have told you my conclusion, Doctor. I repeat it. I think you are making something of nothing."

Dr. Czissar straightened up. "I have given you the facts without prejudice," he said. "Murder has been done. It is clear."

"Not to me, Doctor."

"Very well. I will explain." He cleared his throat, swallowed, and said sharply: "Attention, please!"

Mercer relapsed into his chair. "I can spare you two more minutes, Doctor," he said angrily.

"It will be enough," said Dr. Czissar.

"In the first place, we have the marriage of Mrs. Pewsey and Mr. Stenson. It is the second mistake they have made. It is a fact that asks questions. There is no doubt that they had been having an affair together for very many months. I think that they must have made up their minds to murder the Captain very early on. Mrs. Falcon says that her brother wrote to her nearly a year ago saying that his wife had asked for a divorce and that he had refused. I think we shall find that it was very soon after that that Mr. Stenson bought a life insurance policy from the Captain and became so strangely friendly with him. If we wish for more evidence of the affair, I think that we shall find it at the Hotel Metropolis. It was there that the two were seen after their marriage. Doubtless they had been there many times before. So stupid of them to get married so soon after the murder.

"But you are impatient. We come to the murder. The first thing that is curious is this heart trouble of the Captain's. It was not serious enough to kill. The doctor did not think so. He insisted upon an autopsy. But"—Dr. Czissar raised a cautionary finger—"he performed the autopsy himself without consulting the coroner. As I understand English law, he was within his rights if he had the permission of Mrs. Pewsey; but what is the value of his autopsy? Great experience is necessary in cases when the cause of death is not reasonably obvious."

Mercer grunted.

"Next," pursued Dr. Czissar, "let us consider the manner of the Captain's death. According to the maid, he behaved in an unusual manner. He stumbled and staggered. Now, Assistant-Commissioner, I, too, find that unusual. The Captain was a habitual heavy drinker. In my experience, I have found that such men do *not* usually stumble and stagger from the effects of drink. The Captain was stumbling and staggering. The cause of death was respiratory failure.

What is the link between those two facts? I will tell you. It is the word 'Socrates.'"

"What?"

"You have heard of Socrates, Assistant-Commissioner? Ah, yes. Then you may remember the description of his death. For a time he walks about, then his steps become difficult. Paralysis begins to creep up his legs. He is forced to lie down. The paralysis creeps higher to his chest. And then he dies—of a respiratory failure—paralysis of the lungs. There is only one poison which has that effect. It is the poison which was given to Socrates."

"You mean hemlock! But . . ."

"Hemlock is the name of the plant from which it is obtained, Assistant-Commissioner. The actual poison is coniine. If the coniine is pure and concentrated, a few drops kill very quickly. An ordinary infusion of hemlock leaves would kill, unless treatment were given, in from two to three hours. There are, I find, quantities of hemlock growing in Mr. Stenson's garden. There is no doubt, I think, that when the Captain went into Mr. Stenson's house that night, he was given with his whisky an infusion of hemlock leaves. He had been drinking all the evening. He would not notice the taste. But Mr. Stenson made the first mistake. He has a sense of humor. He was nervous and worried. He was not used to murder. He turned to his sense of humor for comfort. He tried to make a joke of the situation. He called the Captain 'Socrates.'"

"But, good heavens, man!" exploded Mercer, "even if this story is true, how on earth are we going to prove it?"

Dr. Czissar got to his feet with dignity. "I am sure

that you will find a way. Coniine remains detectable in the body for many months. An exhumation and an autopsy by an experienced pathologist with no preconceived ideas about cardiac weakness should help you. You will not, I think, be able to prove administration, but I have no doubt that you will be able to build up a circumstantial case strong enough to convict."

"But what about the woman?" demanded Mercer. "You said that '*they*' did the murder."

"Oh, yes. Mrs. Pewsey was certainly an accessory before the fact. There is no doubt in my mind that it was she who prepared the way for the death certificate by sending her husband to the doctor a week before his death. It is not difficult to upset a drinker's heart. Aspirin tablets are almost tasteless dissolved in soda-water. But you may have difficulty in proving anything against her.

"It is Mr. Stenson for whom I am sorry," he went on. "I have heard so much about the English sense of humor. Now I understand it. I did not think that it would be so macabre, but I like it. It is piquant. Socrates!" He emitted an apologetic little giggle. "It is really very funny."

VI / The Case of the Gentleman Poet

It was after the murderer of Felton Spenser had been tried and convicted that Assistant-Commissioner Mercer finally became resigned to the occasional intrusions of Dr. Jan Czissar into the affairs of his department at New Scotland Yard. For that reason alone, the case would be worth reporting. The conversion of an Assistant-Commissioner of New Scotland Yard into an ordinary human being must be reckoned a major triumph of the power of reason over the force of habit. But the case has another claim to the interest of students of criminology in general and, in particular, of those who contemplate committing murders of their own. It demonstrated clearly that the first requisite for the committal of a perfect murder is the omniscience of a god.

The world first heard of the death of Felton Spenser late one January evening, and through the medium of one of the B.B.C.'s news bulletins. "We regret," said the announcer, in funereal tones, "to announce the death in London tonight of Mr. Felton Spenser, the poet. He was fifty-three. Although Mr. Spenser was born in Manchester, the early years of his life were spent in the county of Flint, and it was in praise of the Flint countryside and scenery that much of his poetry was written. His first collection of poems, 'The Merciful Light,' was published in nineteen-hundred and nine. Mr. Marshall Grieve, the critic and a friend of Spenser's, said of him to-night: 'He was a gentleman in the Edwardian sense of the word. He was a man without enemies. His verse had a placid limpidity rarely met with nowadays, and it flowed with the lyrical ease of his beloved Dee.'"

That was all. It was left to the morning newspapers to disclose the fact that Felton Spenser had been found by his friend, Mr. Marshall Grieve, "the author-critic," shot in his Bloomsbury flat, that there had been a revolver by his side, and that he had recently been suffering from fits of depression. To Assistant-Commissioner Mercer, Detective-Inspector Denton ultimately brought further details.

Felton Spenser had lived in the top flat of a converted house. There were three other flats below his. That on the ground-floor was occupied by a dressmaker and her husband, named Lobb. On the first floor lived Mr. Marshall Grieve. The second floor was unoccupied. The dead man's flat consisted of two large rooms, used as bedroom and sitting-room respectively, a smaller room used as a study, a kitchen, and a bathroom. It had been in the sitting-room that his body had been found.

At about six-thirty that evening, the sound of a shot had come from the top of the house. The dressmaker's husband, Mr. Lobb, who had just returned home from his work, ran to the door of his flat. At the same moment, Mr. Grieve, who had also heard the shot, had appeared at his door at the head of the first flight of stairs. They had gone up together.

After breaking down the door of Felton Spenser's flat, which had a patent lock on it, they had found Spenser half-sitting, half-lying on the sofa, his arms extended, and his hands turned back as though he had, in the throes of death, gripped the edge of the sofa. The body had been rendered rigid by a cadaveric spasm. The appearance of the wound suggested that when the shot had been fired, the revolver had been within an inch or two of the head.

Grieve stated that Spenser had been suffering for some time from fits of intense depression. He knew of several possible causes of these fits. Spenser had been profoundly disappointed by the reception accorded to a book of his poems published the year before. He had also been in financial difficulties. He had never earned a living from his work, and had lived on a small private income left to him by his wife. He had, however, Grieve believed, been speculating with his capital. He had also lent large sums of money to friends. Grieve had seen him earlier in the day of his death. Spenser had then told him that his affairs were in a bad way, and that he was seeing his solicitor the following day in an effort to salvage some of his losses. This statement was confirmed by the solicitor in question. Shortly before five o'clock in the afternoon of the day on which Spenser had died, he had received a telephone call from Spenser, who asked for an appointment for the following day.

The revolver, reported Denton, was an old pin-fire weapon of French manufacture, and unregistered. Spenser could have come by it in a variety of ways. The same applied to the ammunition. Only one shot had been fired from the revolver. The markings on the bullet extracted from the dead man's head showed that it had come from that particular revolver. The only distinguishing feature about the weapon was a series of marks near the muzzle which suggested that at some time a silencer had been fitted to it. There had been no silencer found in the flat. According to the medical report, the wound showed every sign of having been self-inflicted.

There was, in Denton's opinion, only one curious thing about the case. That thing was the draft of an unfinished letter lying on the desk in the study. It was written in pencil, and much corrected, as if the writer had been choosing his words very carefully. It began:

"As I told you yesterday, I was serious when I said that unless the money was repaid to me by to-day I would place the matter in the hands of my legal advisers. You have seen fit to ignore my offer. Accordingly, I have approached my solicitor. Need I say that, if I could afford to overlook the whole unpleasant matter, I would do so eagerly? In asking for the return of the money, I . . ." There the letter stopped.

Mercer considered it. "Looks pretty straightforward to me," he said at last. "According to Grieve, he'd been in the habit of lending people money. It looks as though, having found himself hard pressed, he was trying to get a little of it back. What does his banking account show?"

Denton referred to his notes. "Well, Sir, he'd certainly got rid of some money. He'd bought one or two parcels of doubtful shares, and lost a bit that way. Six months ago he drew out five hundred in cash. Maybe that was this loan he was trying to get back. Funny idea, though, paying it out in cash. I couldn't find any note of who had it, either. By the look of his place, I should say he was the sort who lights his pipe with important papers. But I thought that letter was a bit curious, Sir. Why should he get up in the middle of writing a letter and shoot himself?"

Mercer pursed his lips. "Ever heard of impulse, Denton? That's how half the suicides happen. 'Suicide while the balance of his mind was disturbed,' is the formula. Any life insurance?"

"Not that we can trace, Sir. There's a cousin in Flint who inherits. Executors are Grieve and the solicitor."

"Grieve's important. What sort of witness will he make?"

"Good, Sir. He looks and talks like an archbishop."

"All right, Denton. I'll leave it to you."

And to Denton it was left—for the moment. It was not until the day before the inquest was due to be held that Dr. Czissar sent his card into Mercer's office.

For once, Mercer's excuse that he was too busy to see Dr. Czissar was genuine. He was due at a conference with the Commissioner and it was to Denton that he handed over the job of dealing with the refugee Czech detective.

Again and again during the subsequent conference he wished that he had asked the Doctor to wait, and interviewed him himself. Since the first occasion on which Dr. Czissar had entered New Scotland Yard armed with a letter of introduction from an influential Home Office politician, he had visited Mercer four times. And on every occasion he had brought disaster with him: disaster in the shape of irrefutable proof that he, Dr. Czissar, could be right about a case when Assistant-Commissioner Mercer was hopelessly wrong.

When at last he returned to his office, Denton was waiting for him, and the expression of exasperated resignation on Denton's face told him all he wanted to know about Dr. Czissar's visit. The worst had happened again. The only thing he could do now was to put as stony a face as possible on the impending humiliation. He set his teeth.

"Ah, Denton!" He bustled over to his desk. "Have you got rid of Dr. Czissar?"

Denton squared his shoulders. "No, Sir," he said woodenly. "He's waiting downstairs to see you."

"But I told you to see him."

"I have seen him, Sir. But when I heard what he had to say I thought I'd better keep him here until you were free. It is about this Spenser business, Sir. I'm afraid I've tripped up badly. It's murder."

Mercer sat down carefully. "You mean, I suppose, that it's Dr. Czissar's *opinion* it was murder?"

"No question of opinion, I'm afraid, Sir. A clear case. He got hold of some of the evidence from that journalist friend of his who lends him his Press pass. I've given him the rest. He saw through the whole thing at once. If I'd have had any gumption I'd have seen through it too. He's darn clever."

Mercer choked down the words that rose to his lips. "All right," he said; "you'd better bring Dr. Czissar up."

Dr. Czissar entered the room exactly as he had entered it many times before—thousands of times, it seemed to Mercer. Inside the door, he clicked his heels, clapped his umbrella to his side as if it were a rifle, bowed, and announced loudly: "Dr. Jan Czissar. Late Prague police. At your service!"

To Mercer it was as familiar as the strains of a

detested melody. He said formally: "How do you do, Doctor? I hear that you have something to tell us about the Spenser case."

Dr. Czissar's pale face relaxed. His tall, plump body drooped into its accustomed position beneath the long, drab raincoat. His brown, cow-like eyes beamed through the thick pebble spectacles. "You are busy," he said apologetically. "It is a small matter."

"I understand you think that Mr. Felton Spenser was murdered."

The cow-like eyes enlarged. "Oh, yes. That is what I think, Assistant-Commissioner Mercer. I was a little uncertain as to whether I should come to you about it. The facts on which I base the conclusion I learned from a journalist who tells me things that will interest me for the book I am writing. It is a work of medical jurisprudence. But until Inspector Denton told me that my information was accurate, I was doubtful. You see, it is most important to be accurate in these matters. I was told that the body had been found in a state of cadaveric spasm, and that the revolver was on the floor beside the sofa. The spasm was described to me. I was also told that the finger-prints on the revolver were smeared and indefinite. From the information at my disposal, I had no doubt that Mr. Spenser was murdered."

"And may I ask why, Doctor?"

Dr. Czissar cleared his throat and swallowed hard. "Cadaveric spasm," he declaimed, as if he were addressing a group of students, "is a sudden tightening of the muscles of the body at the moment of death, which produces a rigidity which remains until it is succeeded by the lesser rigidity of *rigor mortis*. The limbs of the dead person will thus remain in the positions in which they were immediately before death for some time. Cadaveric spasm occurs most frequently when the cause of death is accompanied by some violent disturbance of the nervous system. In many cases of suicide by shooting through the head, the weapon is held so tightly by the cadaveric spasm in the dead hand that great force is required to remove it."

Mercer gave a twisted smile. "And although there was a cadaveric spasm, the revolver was found on the floor. Is that your point? I'm afraid, Doctor, that we can't accept that as proof of murder. A cadaveric spasm may relax after quite a short time. The fact that the hand had not actually retained the weapon is not proof that it did not fire it. So—"

"Precisely," interrupted Dr. Czissar. "But that was *not* my point, Assistant-Commissioner. According to the medical report, about which the Inspector has been good enough to tell me, the body was in a state of unrelaxed cadaveric spasm when it was examined an hour after it was discovered. The fingers of both hands were slightly crooked, and both hands were drawn backwards almost at right angles to the forearms. But let us think"—he drove one la[illegible] finger into his right temple—"let us think about the effect of a cadaveric spasm. It locks the muscles in the position assumed immediately before death. Very well, then. Mr. Spenser's right hand immediately before his death was drawn backwards almost at right-angles to the forearm. Also, the fingers of that hand were slightly crooked. It is not possible, Assistant-Commissioner Mercer, to hold a revolver to the head and pull the trigger with the hand in that position."

Mercer looked sharply at Denton. "You saw the body before it was moved. Do you agree with this?"

"I'm afraid I do, Sir," said Denton dejectedly. "I ought to have spotted it for myself, but I'm afraid I don't know much about how spasms work."

"It is not expected that you should, Inspector," said Dr. Czissar kindly. "These things must be learned. But there is, I think, another conclusion to be drawn from the position of the hands. There is no doubt that Mr. Spenser was in the act of rising from the sofa when he was shot. His hands bent in that way could only have been used to raise himself so that he could stand up. The peculiar position of the body thus becomes quite clear."

"Everything, in fact, becomes quite clear," snarled Mercer, "except the identity of the murderer."

The cow-like eyes gleamed. "That also is clear, Assistant-Commissioner. As soon as Inspector Denton informed me of the evidence available, I was able to see what had happened."

Mercer contained himself with an effort. "And what *did* happen?"

A thin smile stretched the Doctor's full lips. He straightened his back, cleared his throat, swallowed hard, and said sharply, "Attention, please!"

Of all Dr. Czissar's mannerisms, it was the one that irritated Mercer most. He sat back in his chair. "Well, Doctor?"

"In the first place," said Dr. Czissar, "we have to consider the fact that, on the evidence of the dressmaker, no one left the house after Mr. Spenser was killed. Therefore, when the police arrived the murderer was still there. Inspector Denton tells me also that the entire house, including the empty flat on the second floor, was searched by the police. Therefore, the murderer was one of the three persons in the house at the time—the dressmaker, Mrs. Lobb, her husband, who returned home before the shot was heard, and Mr. Grieve. But which?

"Mr. Lobb states that, on hearing the shot, he ran to the door of his flat and looked up the stairs, where he saw Mr. Grieve appear at the door of his flat. They then went up together to the scene of the crime. If both these men are innocent and telling the truth, then there is an absurdity: for if neither of them shot Mr. Spenser, then Mrs. Lobb shot him, although she was downstairs at the time of the shot. It is not possible. Nor is it possible for either of the men to have shot him, unless they are both lying. Another absurdity. We are faced with the conclusion that someone has been ingenious.

"How was the murder committed?" Dr. Czissar's cow-like eyes sought piteously for understanding. "How? There is only one clue in our possession. It is that a microscopic examination of the revolver-barrel showed Inspector Denton that at some time a silencer had been fitted to it. Yet no silencer is found in Mr. Spenser's flat. We should not expect to find it, for the revolver probably belongs to the murderer. Perhaps the murderer has the silencer? I think so. For only then can we explain the fact that when a shot is heard, none of the suspects is in Mr. Spenser's room."

"But," snapped Mercer, "if a silencer had been fitted, the shot would not have been heard. It *was* heard."

Dr. Czissar smiled. "Therefore, we must conclude that two shots were fired, one to kill, the other to be heard."

"But only one shot had been fired from the revolver that killed Spenser."

"Oh, yes, Assistant-Commissioner, that is true. But the murder was, I believe, committed with two revolvers. I believe that Mr. Grieve went to Mr. Spenser's flat, armed with the revolver you found, at about six o'clock, or perhaps earlier. There was a silencer fitted to the revolver, and when the opportunity came, he shot Mr. Spenser through the head. He then removed the silencer, smudged the finger-prints on the revolver and left it by Mr. Spenser on the floor. He then returned to his own flat and hid the silencer. The next thing he did was to wait until Mr. Lobb returned home, take a second revolver, go up into the empty flat, and fire a second, but blank, shot.

"Mr. Lobb—he will be the most valuable witness for the prosecution—says in his evidence that, on hearing the shot, he ran to his door and saw Mr. Grieve coming out of his flat. It sounds very quick of him, but I think it must have taken Mr. Lobb longer than he thinks. He would, perhaps, look at his wife, ask her what the noise was, and *then* go to his door. Yet even a few seconds would be time for Mr. Grieve to fire the shot, descend one short flight of stairs, and pretend to be coming out of his door."

"I gathered that you had Grieve in mind," said Mercer, "but may I remind you that this is all supposition? Where is the proof? What was Grieve's motive?"

"The proof," said Dr. Czissar comfortably, "you will find in Mr. Grieve's flat—the silencer, the second revolver, and perhaps pin-fire ammunition. He will not have got rid of these things for fear of being seen doing so. Also, I suggest that Mr. Lobb, the dressmaker's husband, be asked to sit in his room and listen to two shots: one fired in Mr. Spenser's room from the revolver that killed Mr. Spenser, the other, a blank shot, fired in the empty flat. You will find, I think, that he will swear that it was the second shot he heard. The two noises will be quite different.

"For the motive, I suggest that you consider Mr. Grieve's financial arrangements. Some months ago, Mr. Spenser drew five hundred pounds in cash from his bank. There is no doubt, I think, that Mr. Grieve had it. While we were waiting for you, Assistant-Commissioner, I suggested to the Inspector that some information about Mr. Grieve's income would be helpful. Mr. Grieve, we find, earns a little money writing for a weekly journal. He is also an undischarged bankrupt. He would therefore prefer to receive so large a sum in notes instead of by check. Also, we have only his word that Mr. Spenser lent money freely. I have no doubt that Mr. Grieve obtained the money to invest on Mr. Spenser's behalf, and that he took it for himself. Perhaps you will find some of it in his flat. Mr. Spenser had discovered the theft, and threatened to expose him. The letter he was writing was to Mr. Grieve. But Mr. Grieve did not wait to receive it. He decided to kill Mr. Spenser. The fact that he had this old revolver and silencer no doubt suggested the method. But, like all other clever criminals, he is stupid. He makes a statement about his dead friend. 'A man without enemies,' he says. So strange to comment on the fact, one thinks. So few of us have enemies. But when we see that Mr. Grieve wishes it to be thought that his friend suicided himself, we understand."

Dr. Czissar sighed and stood up. "So kind of you to

receive me, Assistant-Commissioner Mercer. Good afternoon."

"One moment, Doctor."

Mercer had risen to his feet. There was nothing left for him to say that would change the fact of his defeat, and he knew it. The hope that Dr. Czissar would one day prove that he was no more infallible than other men had been deferred too often for him to derive any comfort from it. He did the only thing he could do under the circumstances.

"We're very much obliged to you, Doctor," he said. "We'll always be glad of any help you can give us."

Dr. Czissar's pale face reddened. "You are too kind," he stammered. And then, for once, his English deserted him. "It is to me a great . . ." he began, and then stopped. "It is for me . . ." he said again. He could get no further, and abandoned the attempt to do so. Crimson in the face, he clicked his heels at each of them in turn. "An honor," he said.

Then he was gone. "He's left his umbrella behind," said Denton. "Maybe he'll come back for it."

The Blood Bargain

Ex-President Fuentes enjoys a peculiar distinction. More people would like to kill him now that he is in retirement than wanted to kill him when he was in power.

He is a puzzled and indignant man.

What he fails to understand is that, while men like General Perez may in time forgive you for robbing them, they will never forgive you for making them look foolish.

The *coup d'état* that overthrew Fuentes' Social Action Party government was well organized and relatively bloodless.

The leaders of the *coup* were mostly Army officers, but they had understandings with fellow-dissidents in the Air Force and Navy as well as the discreet blessing of the Church. A price for the collaboration of the Chief of Police had been agreed upon well in advance, and the lists of certain left-wing deputies, militant trade union officials, pro-government newspaper editors, Castro-trained subversives, and other undesirables whose prompt arrest would be advisable, had been compiled with his help. Similar arrangements had been made in the larger provincial towns. Although the conspirators were by no means all of the same political complexion, they had for once found themselves able to sink their differences in the pursuit of a common goal. Whatever might come afterwards, they were all agreed upon one thing; if the country were to be saved from corruption, Communist subversion, anarchy, bankruptcy, civil war, and, ultimately, foreign military intervention, President Fuentes had to go.

One evening in September he went.

The tactics employed by the "Liberation Front" conspirators followed the pattern that has become more or less traditional when a *coup* is backed by organized military forces and opposed, if it is opposed at all, only by civilian mobs and confused, lightly armed garrison units.

As darkness fell, the tanks of two armored brigades together with trucks containing a parachute regiment, signals units, and a company of combat engineers rolled into the capital. Within little more than an hour, they had secured their major objectives. Meanwhile, the Air Force had taken over the international airport, grounded all planes, and established a headquarters in the customs and immigration building. An infantry division now began to move into the city and take up positions that would enable it to deal with the civil disturbances that were expected to develop as news of the *coup*, and of the mass arrests that were accompanying it, reached the densely populated slum areas with their high concentration of Fuentes supporters.

A little after eight-thirty a squadron of tanks and a special task force of paratroopers reached the Presidential Palace. The palace guard resisted for a quarter of an hour and suffered casualties of eight wounded. The order to surrender was given personally to the guard commander by President Fuentes "in order to avoid further bloodshed."

When this was reported to General Perez, the leader of the *coup*, he drove to the Palace. He was accompanied by five senior members of the Liberation Front council, including the Chief of Police, and no less than three representatives of the foreign press. The latter had been flushed out of the Jockey Club bar by an aide earlier in the evening and hastily briefed on the aims and ideals of the Liberation Front. General Perez wished to lose no time in establishing himself abroad as a magnanimous, reasonable, and responsible man, and his regime as worthy of prompt diplomatic recognition.

The newsmen's accounts of the interview between President Fuentes and General Perez, and of the now-notorious "blood bargain" that emerged from it, were all in substantial agreement. At the time the bargain seemed to them just another of those civilized, oddly chivalrous agreements to live and let live which, by testifying to the continued presence of compassion and good sense even at moments of turmoil and destruction, have so often lightened the long, dark history of Latin American revolution. The reporters, all experienced men, can scarcely be blamed for misunderstanding it. They knew, as everyone else knew, that President Fuentes was a devious and deeply dishonest man. The only mistake they made was in assuming that the other parties to the bargain had made due allowance for that deviousness and dishonesty and knew exactly what they were doing. What the reporters had not realized was that these normally wary and hard-headed officers had become so intoxicated by the speed and extent of their initial success that by the time they reached the Presidential Palace they were no longer capable of thinking clearly.

President Fuentes received General Perez and the other Liberation Front leaders in the ornate Cabinet Room of the Palace to which he had been taken by the paratroopers who had arrested him. With him were the other male occupants of the Presidential air raid shelter at the time of his arrest. These included the Palace guard commander, the President's valet, the Palace major domo, two footmen and the man who looked after the Palace plumbing system, in addition to the Minister of Public Welfare, the Minister of Agrarian Education, the Minister of Justice, and the elderly Controller of the Presidential Secretariat. The Minister of Public Welfare had brought a bottle of brandy with him from the shelter and smiled glassily throughout the subsequent confrontation. Agrarian Education and Justice maintained expressions of bewilderment and indignation, but confined their oral protests to circumspect murmurs. The thin-lipped young captain in charge of the paratroopers handled his machine pistol as if he would have been glad of an excuse to use it.

Only the President seemed at ease. There was even a touch of impatience in the shrug with which he rose to face General Perez and his party as they strode in from the anteroom; it was as if he had been interrupted by some importunate visitor during a game of bridge.

His calm was only partly assumed. He knew all about General Perez' sensitivity to foreign opinion, and he had immediately recognized the newsmen in the rear of the procession. They would not have been brought there if any immediate violence to his person had been contemplated.

The impatience he displayed was certainly genuine; it was impatience with himself. He had known for weeks that a *coup* was in preparation, and had taken the precaution a month earlier of sending his wife and children and his mistress out of the country. They were all now in Washington, and he had planned, using as a pretext his announced wish to address personally a meeting of the Organization of American States, to join them there the following week. His private spies had reported that the *coup* would undoubtedly be timed to take advantage of his absence abroad. Since the *coup* by means of which he himself had come to power five years earlier had been timed in that way, he had been disposed to believe the report.

Now, he knew better. Whether or not his spies had deliberately deceived him did not matter at the moment. A mistake had been made which was, he knew, likely to cost him more than temporary inconvenience. Unless he could retrieve it immediately, by getting out of the country within the next few hours, that mistake would certainly cost him his liberty, and most probably his life too.

He had risked death before, was familiar with the physical and mental sensations that accompanied the experience, and with a small effort was able to ignore them. As General Perez came up to him, the President displayed no emotion of any kind. He merely nodded politely and waited for the General to speak.

For a moment the General seemed tongue-tied. He was sweating too. As this was the first time he had overthrown a government he was undoubtedly suffering from stage fright. He took refuge finally in military punctilio. With a click of the heels he came to attention and fixed his eyes on the President's left ear.

"We are here . . ." he began harshly, then cleared his throat and corrected himself. "I and my fellow members of the Council of the Liberation Front are here to inform you that a state of national emergency now exists."

The President nodded politely. "I am glad to have that information, General. Since telephone communication has been cut off I have naturally been curious as to what was happening. These gentlemen"—he motioned to the paratroopers—"seemed unwilling to enlighten me."

The General ignored this and went on as if he were reading a proclamation. In fact, he was quoting from the press release which had already been handed to the newsmen. "Directed by the Council and under its orders," he said, "the armed forces have assumed control of all functions of civil government in the state, and, as provided in the Constitution, formally demand your resignation."

The President looked astounded. "You have the effrontery to claim constitutional justification for this mutiny?"

For the first time since he had entered the room the General relaxed slightly. "We have a precedent, sir. Nobody should know that better than you. You yourself set it when you legalized your own seizure of power from your predecessor. Need I remind you of the wording of the amendment? 'If for any reason, including the inability to fulfill the duties of his office by reason of ill health, mental or physical, or absence, an elected president is unable to exercise the authority vested in him under the constitution, a committee representative of the nation and those responsible to it for the maintenance of law and order may request his resignation and be entitled . . .'"

For several seconds the President had been waving his hands for silence. Now he broke in angrily. "Yes, yes, I know all about that. But my predecessor was absent. I am not. Neither am I ill, physically or mentally. There are no legal grounds on which you are entitled to ask for my resignation."

"No legal grounds, sir?" General Perez could smile now. He pointed to the paratroopers. "Are you able to exercise the authority of a president? *Are* you? If you think so, try."

The President pretended to think over the challenge. The interview was so far going more or less as he had expected; but the next moves would be the critical ones for him. He walked over to a window and back in order to give himself time to collect himself.

Everyone there was watching him. The tension in the room was mounting. He could feel it. It was odd, he thought. Here he was, a prisoner, wholly at their mercy; and yet they were waiting for him to come to a decision, to make a choice where no choice existed. It was absurd. All they wanted from him was relief from a small and quite irrational sense of guilt. They had the Church's blessing; now the poor fools yearned for the blessing of the law too. Very well. They should have it. But it would be expensive.

He turned and faced General Perez again.

"A resignation exacted from me under duress would have no force in law," he said.

The General glanced at the Chief of Police. "You are a lawyer, Raymundo. Who represents the law here?"

"The Council of the Liberation Front, General."

Perez looked at the President again. "You see, sir, there are no technical difficulties. We even have the necessary document already prepared."

His aide held up a black leather portfolio.

The President hesitated, looking from one face to another as if hoping against hope that he might find a friendly one. Finally he shrugged. "I will read the document," he said coldly and walked toward the cabinet table. As he did so he seemed to become aware again of his fellow prisoners in the room. He stopped suddenly.

"Must my humiliation be witnessed by my colleagues and my servants as well as the foreign press?" he demanded bitterly.

General Perez motioned to the paratrooper captain. "Take those men into another room. Leave guards outside the doors of this one."

The President waited until the group from the air raid shelter had been herded out, then sat down at the table. The General's aide opened the portfolio, took out a legal document laced with green ribbon and placed it in front of the President.

He made a show of studying the document very carefully. In fact, he was indifferent to its contents. His intention was simply to let the tension mount a little further and to allow the other men there to feel that they were on the point of getting what they wanted.

For three minutes there was dead silence in the room. It was broken only by the sound of distant machine-gun fire. It seemed to be coming from the south side of the city. The President heard a slight stir from the group of men behind him and one of them cleared his throat nervously. There was another burst of firing. The President took no notice of it. He read the document through a third time then put it down and sat back in his chair.

The aide offered him a pen with which to sign. The President ignored it and turned his head so that he could see General Perez.

"You spoke of a resignation, General," he said. "You did not mention that it was to be a confession also."

"Hardly a confession, sir," the General replied drily. "We would not expect you voluntarily to incriminate yourself. The admission is only of incompetence. That is not yet a criminal offence in a head of state."

The President smiled faintly. "And if I were to sign this paper, what kind of personal treatment might I expect to receive afterwards? A prison cell perhaps, with a carefully staged treason trial to follow? Or merely a bullet in the head and an unmarked grave?"

The General reddened. "We are here to correct abuses of power, sir, not to imitate them. When you have signed you will be conducted to your former home in Alazan province. You will be expected to remain there for the present and the Governor of the province will be instructed to see that you do so. Apart from that restriction you will be free to do as you please. Your family will naturally be permitted to join you."

"You mention the house in Alazan province. What about my other personal property?"

"You will be permitted to retain everything you owned when you took office."

"I see." The President stood up and moved away from the table. "I will think about it. I will let you have my decision tomorrow," he added casually.

The silence that followed this announcement did not last long, but one of the newsmen reported later that it was one of the loudest he had ever heard. Another remembered that during it he suddenly became conscious of the presence and smell of a large bowl of tropical flowers on a side table by the anteroom door.

The President had walked towards the windows again. General Perez took two steps towards him, then stopped.

"You must decide at once! You must sign now!" he snapped.

The President turned on him. "Why? Why now?"

It was the Chief of Police who answered him. "Son of a whore, because we tell you to!" he shouted.

Suddenly they were all shouting at him. One officer was so enraged that he drew his pistol. The General had difficulty in restoring order.

The President took no notice of them. He kept his eyes on General Perez, but it was really the newsmen he was addressing now. As the din subsided he raised his voice.

"I asked a question, General. Why now? Why the haste? It is a reasonable question. If, as you say, you already control the country, what have you to fear from me? Or is it, perhaps, that your control is not in fact as complete and effective as you would have us believe?"

The General had to quell another angry outburst from his colleagues before he could answer, but he preserved his own temper admirably. His reply was calm and deliberate.

"I will tell you exactly what we control so that you may judge for yourself," he said. "To begin with all provincial army garrisons, air force establishments, and police posts have declared for the Liberation Front, as have five out of eight of the provincial governors. The three objectors—I am sure you will have guessed who they are—have been rendered harmless and replaced by military governors. None of this can come as a great surprise to you, I imagine. You never had much support outside the capital and the mining areas."

The President nodded. "Stupidity can sometimes be charted geographically," he remarked.

"Now as to the capital. We control the airfields, both military and civil, the naval base, all communications including telephone and radio and television broadcast facilities, the power stations, all fuel oil storage facilities, all main traffic arteries, all government offices and city police posts together with the offices and printing presses of *El Correo* and *La Gaceta*." He glanced at his watch. "In connection with the broadcast facilities, I may mention that while the television station is temporarily off the air, the radio station will shortly begin broadcasting an announcement of the establishment of the new Liberation Front regime, which I recorded two days ago. As I told you before, everything is now under our control."

The President smiled and glanced significantly at

the newsmen. "Are the *sumideri* under control, General?"

Sumideri, meaning sinks or drains, was the popular slang term used to describe the slum areas on the south side of the capital.

The General hesitated only an instant. "The southern area is effectively contained," he replied stiffly. "The first infantry division reinforced by the third tank brigade has that responsibility."

"I see." The President looked again at the newsmen. "So the civil war may be expected to begin at any moment."

With a quick motion of his hands the General silenced the chorus of objections from his colleagues. "We are fully prepared to deal firmly with any mob violence which may occur," he said. "Of that you may be sure."

"Yes," said the President bitterly, "perhaps civil war is not the phrase to use for the planned massacre of unarmed civilians." He swung around suddenly to face the newsmen and his voice hardened. "You have been witnesses to this farce, gentlemen. I ask you to remember it well and let the civilized world know of it. These men come to ask for my resignation as head of state. That is all they want! Why? Because outside in the streets of the city their tanks and guns are waiting to begin the slaughter of the thousands of men and women who will protest their loyalty to me. And the way to bring them out for the slaughter is to fling my resignation like so much filth in their faces!"

General Perez could stand it no longer. "That is a lie!" he shouted.

The President turned on him savagely. "Do you think they will *not* come out? Why else are they 'contained' as you call it? Why else? Because they are my people and because they will listen only to me."

A glow of triumph suffused General Perez' angry face. "Then their blood will be on *your* hands!" he roared. He stabbed a forefinger at the newsmen. "You heard what he said, gentlemen. *They do what he tells them!* It is his responsibility, then, not ours, if they oppose us. *He* will be the murderer of women and children! Let him deny it."

This time the President made no reply. He just stood there looking about him in bewilderment, like a boxer who has staggered to his feet after a count of ten and can't quite realize that the fight is over. At last he walked slowly back to the cabinet table, sat down heavily, and buried his head in his hands.

Nobody else moved. When the President raised his head and looked at them again his eyes were haggard. He spoke very quietly.

"You are right," he said, "they are my people and they will do as I tell them. It is my responsibility. I accept it. There must be no senseless bloodshed. I think it is my duty to tell them not to protest."

For a moment they all stared at him incredulously. The Chief of Police started to say something, then stopped as he caught General Perez' eye. If the man were serious this was too good an opportunity to miss.

General Perez went over and addressed the President. "I cannot believe that even you would speak lightly on such a matter, but I must ask if you seriously mean what you say?"

The President nodded absently. "I will need about an hour to draft my statement. There is a direct line to the radio station here in the Palace and the necessary equipment. The station can record me on tape." He managed a rueful smile. "In the circumstances, I imagine that you would prefer a recording to a live broadcast."

"Yes." But the General was still reluctant to believe in his triumph. "How can you be sure that they will obey you?" he asked.

The President thought before he answered. "There will be some, of course, who will be too distressed, too angry perhaps, to do as I ask," he said. "But if the officers commanding troops are ordered to use restraint, casualties can be kept to a minimum." He glanced at the Chief of Police. "There should be moderation, too, in respect of arrests. But the majority will listen to me, I think." He paused. "The important thing is that they must believe that I am speaking as a free man, and not out of fear because there is a pistol at my head."

"I myself can give them that assurance," said the General. The fact that he could make such an ingenuous suggestion is an indication of his mental confusion at that point.

The President raised his eyebrows. "With all respect, General, I don't think we could expect them at this time to believe you of all people. I also think that the news that I am to be kept under what amounts to house arrest in Alazan province will not help to convince them either."

"Then what do you propose? You can scarcely remain here in the capital."

"Naturally not." The President sat back in his chair. He had assumed a statesmanlike air now. "It is quite clear," he said, "that we must achieve an orderly and responsible transfer of power. I shall, of course, resign in order to make way for the Liberation Front.

However, in your place, I must say that I would regard my continued presence anywhere in this country as undesirable. These people to whom I am to appeal tonight will only respond with restraint because of their loyalty to me. That loyalty will continue as long as they are able to give expression to it. You would do better really to get rid of me. As soon as I have spoken to my people you should get me out of the country as quickly as you can."

"Exile?" It was the Chief of Police who spoke up now. "But if we exile you that looks no better than house arrest in Alazan. Worse, possibly."

"Exactly." The President nodded approvingly. "The solution I suggest is that I am permitted to announce to my people that I will continue to serve them, the nation, and the Liberation Front, but in a different capacity and abroad. Our embassy in Nicaragua is without an ambassador at present. That would be a suitable appointment. I suggest that after I have recorded my broadcast I leave the country immediately in order to take up my post."

The council discussion that ensued lacked the vehemence of the earlier exchanges. The strain of the past twenty-four hours was beginning to tell on General Perez and his colleagues; they were getting tired; and the sounds of firing from the south side were becoming more insistent. Time was running out. It was one of the newsmen who drew their attention to the fact.

"General," he said to Perez, "has it occurred to you that if the President doesn't talk to these people of his pretty soon they're all going to be out on the streets anyway?"

The President recognized the urgency, too, but

refused to be hurried. As he pointed out, there were matters of protocol to be dealt with before he could make his appeal to the people. For one thing, his resignation would have to be redrafted. Since, he argued, he was now to be appointed his country's Ambassador to Nicaragua, references in the present draft to his incompetence would obviously have to be deleted. And there were other clauses which might be interpreted as reflections on his personal integrity.

In the end, the President wrote his own act of resignation. It was a simple document but composed with great care. His radio speech, on the other hand, he scribbled out on a cabinet desk pad while technicians, hastily summoned by jeep from the central radio building, were setting up a recording circuit in the anteroom.

Meanwhile, telephone communication had been restored to the Palace, and the Controller of the Presidential Secretariat had been released from arrest and put to work in his office.

His first task had been to contact the Nicaraguan Ambassador, give him a discreetly censored account of the current situation and request him to ascertain immediately, in accordance with Article 8 of the Pan-American Convention, if his government would be prepared to accept ex-President Fuentes as *persona grata* in the capacity of ambassador to their country. The Nicaraguan Ambassador had undertaken to telephone personally to the Minister of Foreign Relations in Managua and report back. His unofficial opinion was that there would be no opposition to the proposed appointment.

With the help of the air force council member present the Controller next spoke to the officer in charge at the International Airport. He learned that of the two civil airliners grounded earlier that evening, one had been southbound to Caracas, the other, a Colombian Avianca jet, had been northbound to Mexico City. Fortunately, a Vice-Consul from the Colombian Consulate-General was already at the airport, having been summoned there by the Avianca captain to protest the grounding. The Controller spoke with the Vice-Consul who said that Avianca would be willing to carry ex-President Fuentes as a passenger to Mexico City if the Mexican Government would permit him to land. A call to the Mexican Embassy explaining that ex-President Fuentes would be in transit through Mexican territory on his way to his post as an accredited diplomatic representative to the republic of Nicaragua secured the necessary permission.

The President already had a diplomatic passport which needed only minor amendments to fit it for its new role. All that was needed now to facilitate his departure was confirmation from the Nicaraguan Ambassador that he would be accorded diplomatic status in Managua. Within an hour, the Nicaraguan Government, acting promptly in the belief that they were helping both parties to the arrangement, had replied favorably.

The escape route was open.

President Fuentes made two tape-recordings of the appeal to his supporters, one for the radio, the second for use by a loudspeaker van in the streets of the *sumideri*. Then he signed his resignation and was driven to the airport. General Perez provided an escort of armored cars.

The plane, with ex-President Fuentes on board,

took off a little after midnight. Five hours later it landed in Mexico City.

News of the Liberation Front *coup* and of the President's voluntary resignation and ambassadorial appointment had been carried by all the international wire services, and there were reporters waiting for him. There was also, despite the early hour, a protocol official from the Department of External Relations to meet him. Fuentes made a brief statement to the reporters, confirming the fact of his resignation. On the subject of his appointment as Ambassador to Nicaragua he was vague. He then drove to a hotel in the city. On the way there he asked the protocol official if it would be convenient for him to call upon the Minister of External Affairs later that day.

The official was mildly surprised. As Ambassador Fuentes was merely passing through Mexico, a brief note of thanks to the Minister would normally be the only courtesy expected of him. On the other hand, the circumstances of Fuentes' sudden translation from President to Ambassador were unusual and it was possible that the Minister might be glad of the opportunity of hearing what Fuentes himself had to say on the subject. He promised that he would consult the Minister's personal assistant at the earliest possible moment.

The Minister received Ambassador Fuentes at five o'clock that afternoon.

The two men had met before, at conferences of the Organization of American States and on the occasion of a state visit to Mexico paid by Fuentes soon after he became President. It was a tribute to the Minister's natural courtesy as well as his self-discipline that Fuentes believed that the Minister liked him. In fact the Minister viewed him with dislike and disapproval and had not been in the least surprised or distressed by the news of the Liberation Front *coup*. However, he had been amused by Fuentes' ability to emerge from the situation not only alive and free but also invested with diplomatic immunity; and it modified his distaste for the man. He was, one had to admit, an engaging scoundrel.

After the preliminary politenesses had been disposed of the Minister inquired courteously whether he could be of any service to the Ambassador during his stay in Mexico.

Fuentes inclined his head: "That is most kind of you, Mr. Minister," he said graciously. "Yes, there is one thing."

"You only have to ask."

"Thank you." Ambassador Fuentes straightened up a little in his chair. "I wish," he said, "to make formal application to be considered here as a refugee, and formally to request political asylum in the United States of Mexico."

The Minister stared for a moment, then smiled.

"Surely you must be joking, Mr. Ambassador."

"Not in the least."

The Minister was puzzled, and because he was puzzled he put into words the first obvious objection that came into his head.

"But in the United States of Mexico, even though you are not accredited to the Federal Government, you already, by virtue of the Pan-American Convention, enjoy diplomatic status and privileges here," he said.

It was a statement which he was later to regret.

Ambassador Fuentes never took up his post in Nicaragua.

One of the first official acts of General Perez' Council of the Liberation Front was to set up a committee, headed by the Professor of Political Economy at Bolívar University, to report on the financial state of the Republic.

It took the committee only a few days to discover that during the past three years ex-President Fuentes had authorized printings of five hundred peseta banknotes to a total value of one hundred million dollars and that twenty of those hundred millions could not be accounted for.

The Governor of the National Bank was immediately arrested. He was an old man who had spent most of his life in the National Archives gathering material for a scholarly study of colonial Spanish land grants. He had been appointed to the bank by Fuentes. He knew nothing about banking. He had merely carried out the orders of the Minister of Finance.

Fuentes had been his own Minister of Finance.

Interviewed on the subject by the press in Mexico City, ex-President Fuentes stated that the committee's revelations had shocked, horrified, and amazed him. He also said that he had no idea where the missing twenty million might be. Regrettably, he was unable quite to refrain from smiling as he said it.

Ex-President Fuentes' retirement has not been peaceful.

During the five years he held office as President there was only one serious attempt on his life. Since he resigned the Presidency, ceased to concern himself with politics, and went to live abroad, no less than three such attempts have been made. There will doubtless be others. Meanwhile, he has had to fight off two lots of extradition proceedings and a number of civil actions directed against his European bank accounts.

He is wealthy, of course, and can afford to pay for the protection, both physical and legal, that he needs; but he is by no means resigned to the situation. As he is fond of pointing out, other men in his position have accumulated larger fortunes. Moreover, his regime was never unacceptably oppressive. He was no Trujillo, no Batista, no Porfirio Diaz. Why then should he be hounded and harassed as if he were?

Ex-President Fuentes remains a puzzled and indignant man.